Darkness closed in on her with terrifying completeness.

Keely heard the harsh sound of her breaths in the sudden, awful quiet. Oh, God. Oh, God. She waited for the rest of the kitchen, the rest of her *house,* to fall down on top of her.

Arms she hadn't realized were holding her tightened, as if ready to shield her from anything. She couldn't see a thing, not even the man she was clinging to. She was on top of him, she realized. They'd hit hard, him protecting her with his body.

Something cold and hard stuck out of the waistband of his jeans, beneath the cover of his jacket, as she drew her hands down and away. She felt him freeze, and she moved quickly before he could, grabbed it with one hand and stumbled back, knowing what she held. Not needing any light.

She was holding a gun.

Dear Reader,

As I developed the idea for my HAVEN series, I wanted to create a tiny town where an unusual event could trigger a wave of paranormal activity. What more fundamentally earth-shattering event is there than an earthquake? And what more perfect place could such a series be set but in the wild and preternaturally beautiful mountains of West Virginia? In *Secrets Rising,* Keely Schiffer wants nothing more than to start a new life in her old farmhouse, but her life and her home come crashing down over her head when an earthquake strikes. Add to that a mysterious skull in her rose garden and a strange gift from the grave left behind by her dead husband. She's got enough trouble even without finding herself trapped with a possibly dangerous—and most certainly sexy—stranger, Jake Malloy. Secrets are definitely surfacing, along with something shockingly supernatural, and when they witness the unbelievable together, Jake is the only man she can trust to help her find the truth...before it's too late.

Romantic, emotional, chilling and otherworldly...
Welcome to Haven, West Virginia.

Love,

Suzanne McMinn

Suzanne McMinn

SECRETS RISING

Silhouette®

Romantic

SUSPENSE

SILHOUETTE BOOKS

ISBN-13: 978-0-373-27544-1
ISBN-10:   0-373-27544-7

SECRETS RISING

Visit Silhouette Books at www.eHarlequin.com

Printed in U.S.A.

Books by Suzanne McMinn

Silhouette Romantic Suspense

Her Man To Remember #1324
Cole Dempsey's Back in Town #1360
*The Beast Within #1377
*Third Sight #1392
*Deep Blue #1405
**Secrets Rising #1474

*PAX
**Haven

SUZANNE McMINN

is an award-winning author of two dozen novels, including genres such as contemporary paranormal romance, romantic suspense and contemporary romantic comedy, as well as a medieval trilogy. She lives on a farm in the mountains of West Virginia, where she is plotting her next book and enjoying the simple life with her family, friends and many, many cats. Check out her upcoming books and blog at www.suzannemcminn.com.

In tribute to my great-aunt Ruby
and her farmhouse—my haven.

Chapter 1

There was a skull in her rose bed.

Keely Schiffer swiped the hair out of her eyes, felt the damp, cool smear of fresh dirt she'd applied to her cheek in the process, along with the sensation of her insides starting to crawl. The shovel dropped out of her other hand.

That wasn't *really* a skull, was it? It was probably just a rock. A big one. With gaping eye sockets—

Somebody screamed.

She realized that somebody had been her and that somehow she'd ended up about three feet back without being aware of her feet moving. Yes, that was a skull, a *human* skull. She should call the police. She hated calling the police. She'd called the police too many times lately. And they'd called her too many times to count. That's what happened when your husband had a lot of secrets you didn't know about and then got himself killed doing something stupid—

Oh, God. Was this another one of Ray's secrets?

It was Ray who'd had the bright idea of digging up this bed. *Plant some roses*, he'd said. Then he'd dug the crap out of it, torn out the old boxwood hedges, and left it in a big mess last fall right before—

Keely staggered back a few more steps then forced herself to move forward again to the hole she'd dug. She stood on trembling legs, her heart beating fast. *Do something*.

It took her ten seconds to decide. As if there was a decision to make.

Thunder rumbled in the distance. A sudden whip of wind tore through the West Virginia mountain hollow, buffeting leftover dead leaves from winter across the short grass. Another spring storm was on the way. She wasn't going to get the gorgeous hybrid tea roses planted in time. She wasn't going to get them planted today at all, not until the police were finished.... And she'd been so looking forward to this one day off to play outside in the dirt and sunshine. She looked back at the neatly lined-up roses, ready for planting. They had a short growing season here in the mountain region. She needed to get her bushes planted. That thought had seemed really important just about five minutes ago.

Her head reeled. She ran for the back door of the house, burst inside and reached for the phone. She punched 911 before the reality of the silent air hit her.

The phone was out.

The old house settled still and heavy around her. The farm was five miles outside Haven on a road so narrow, to pass another car one vehicle or the other had to pull over on the weedy shoulder. Sugar Run Farm had been in her family for four generations. It wasn't unusual for the phone to go out, storm or no storm. Inconveniences were par for the course in the boonies. There was no cell signal, no cable. They were lucky to have satellite TV. Dickie the mechanic provided personal service.... Including picking up his customers' vehicles on site then dropping them back off.

The windows on her ten-year-old Ford pickup

weren't operating properly. Dickie had picked it up first thing this morning, promising it back by tonight. No phone. No vehicle. Not too big of a problem normally, especially on her day off.

Except for the skull in her rose bed and some really scary thoughts about how it might have gotten there.

But it wasn't an emergency, was it? It had been there since last fall…. Probably. And she'd been living right here all this time, sleeping soundly in spite of it. No reason for alarm now….

And yet, she was alarmed. Creeped out. She'd never minded being alone all the way out here.

Till now.

Row after row after row of timeworn family photographs stared down at her from the parlor walls as she cradled the portable phone back on its base. Through the large front window, she could see the day darkening swiftly. Wind crackled through the leaves on the two maple trees out front. Rain poured down, then the house gave a sudden shake.

Something crashed in the kitchen.

She ran the short distance, pulse thudding. A large cookie jar shaped like a windmill lay shattered on the floor, jostled off the shelf over the cabinets. Staring down at the broken cream-and-blue ceramic jar, she realized something small and shiny sat in the middle of the shards.

She paused for a long beat, glancing up at the ceiling. Had a tree struck the house? Nothing else made sense…. Dammit, she'd have to go check, make sure there wasn't water coming into the attic just in case it *had* been a tree.

Glancing down again, she reached for the foil-wrapped box. She had a second's instinctive temptation to play the childlike game of shaking it lightly, trying to guess what was inside. Her chest tightened. It was silver Christmas wrap with a tone-on-tone pattern of bells and ribbons, but the peel-and-stick holiday label with the bright caricature of Rudolph the Rednosed Reindeer on one end said Happy Birthday, Baby.

In Ray's writing.

So like Ray to not buy any real birthday wrapping, just use what he found in the house then stick something of possible value where probably even he would have forgotten it.

So not like Ray to buy her a gift that he had to have wrapped six months in advance since he'd died last fall and her birthday was tomorrow….

A pounding had the small wrapped box falling out of her hand and rolling onto the shards. It took her a minute to realize the noise was coming from the door, not the roof. God, she was on edge.

Finding a skull in your rose garden did that to a person. She didn't know whether she wanted to laugh or cry at that thought. As for the gift from the grave from Ray...

That was just weird. And sad. She'd figured out a long time ago that her marriage had been a result of youthful stupidity. But she had loved him nonetheless, in the way you can love a troublesome child, and she was determined to forget and forgive and move on. She hadn't been a perfect wife, either—

Whoever was at the door banged on it again. Impatient. She ran across the slightly slanted parlor floor—the foundation of the one-hundred-year-old farmhouse had shifted off-kilter more years ago than she knew about—and grabbed the handle. The carved wooden door swung inward, revealing a broad-shouldered figure, his profile shadowed on the porch overhang in the storm-darkened afternoon. Rain splattered down behind the man, puddles already forming in the yard. A very late model, very expensive-looking, very not-often-seen-around-these-parts sports car was pulled over and parked under the old oak by the cracked and crumbling concrete walk leading up to the house.

She found herself looking into the deepest green eyes she'd ever seen, fringed with incredible lashes. Near-black hair, on the long side, was plastered to his head, fanning the collar of his T-shirt. He hadn't escaped the burst of rain before he'd made it onto her porch.

"Keely Schiffer?"

He looked—and sounded—a little tense, even angry. Stubble shadowed his strong, well-defined jaw. He was dressed casually in faded jeans with a rip in one knee and a black tee under a leather bomber jacket, but there was nothing laid-back about his hard-edged demeanor.

He looked dangerous. And not in a good mood.

A shiver rippled up her spine and she couldn't decide if it was trepidation or, shockingly, attraction.

"Yes?" *And you are—*

"Jake Malloy," he said without her having to voice that question. "I was up at the Foodway and they said you hadn't left the keys to the Evans house. I was under the impression they would be there for me to pick up. Today."

Now she knew why he was mad. She'd set up the rental last week when he'd called. It was her fault for forgetting to leave the keys as arranged. And very out of character.

"Spring fever must have taken over my brain. I'm so sorry—"

He cut off her attempt at apology. "And I'm wet, miles out of my way, and I have other things to do. Do you have the keys?"

Well, now they had established that he was an ass. Good thing she hadn't noticed that he was also heart-throb material, especially since she was all done with men anyway. Not that she didn't like men. She liked plenty of males, mostly the ones who were related to her and were under the age of twelve. And yet she found herself remembering that she probably had dirt smeared on her face and she definitely had dirt on her jeans and the bright-yellow Haven Honeybees high school booster club T-shirt she was wearing.

He was probably six foot two, which had the effect of making her feel unusually feminine and petite at her five foot eight. That's all it was. And there was that bad-boy heartthrob thing, of course, that made her think of mindless sex.

Mindless sex with a stranger. Hot and raw and wild. One fantasy before she died.

Her pulse raced a little. *Stop it*, she warned her-self. Really, she didn't even *like* him so far and she was thinking about having sex with him? Was she losing her mind? She had enough problems at the moment without making any new ones up.

Like, that skull in her rose bed....

"I'm sorry," she repeated. He could be rude; she couldn't. She had exactly two ways to earn money since Ray died— she'd taken over the small Foodway store in town he'd made the monumental mistake and command decision to mortgage her inheritance against, and she also handled local leasing properties as a sideline. Well, she let one of the neighbors run cattle on the farm and put up hay twice a year. But that didn't cut it, with the farm slipping through her fingers because of the store's sliding profit margin since the big warehouse-style grocery outlet had opened in the next town over last summer. "I have the keys. I forgot to leave them up at the store. I'll get them. It'll just take a sec."

She left him standing there and ran back to the kitchen. "So what kind of work do you do?" she called back to him through the screen. She'd left the main door open. Maybe he couldn't hear her over the rain lashing down, but he didn't answer. She remembered asking him why he was coming to Haven when he'd arranged the lease. He'd changed the subject then. And now—

The keys were on a hook on the wall with a little paper tag that read Evans. The rental house was, in fact, straight across the road from the Foodway, so no doubt he was extra annoyed that he'd had to drive all the way out in the country to find her. Or he was just an impatient ass and if he wasn't pissed off about one thing, he'd be pissed off about another.

She headed back to the door. "What brings you to Haven?"

"Business," he said briefly.

"What kind of business?" Did she really want to know or was she just being passive-aggressive at this point? She wasn't really sure. He didn't want to tell her anything, she was sure of *that*.

"I need to get going if you've got those keys."

She felt as if he'd smacked her hand. And maybe she just didn't really want him to go, even if he was an ass. She'd be alone again, just her and that skull and Ray's gift from the grave.

"Here you go." She leaned out between the doorjamb and the screen door just enough to pass him the keys. Their fingers brushed oh-so-briefly and she told herself to ignore the crackle of waking female libido that had no place in her life.

He was good-looking—so what? Good-looking

and a little secretive. Even if she was interested in dating, which she was not, she'd had enough of the mysterious type. And he was surly to boot. And really, maybe he was a criminal. Drug activity had leaked out of the city, into rural communities. Maybe he was a thug. He certainly looked like one.

"My phone's out," she went on. "So if you tried to call from the store—" Not that she would have been able to drive the keys up there anyway since she didn't have her truck.

"Thanks for the keys." He didn't sound like he meant that and he was already turning away.

"Wait!" Keely bit her lip. How was she supposed to say this? "My phone is out, like I said, and my truck is in the shop—"

He stood there, still looking annoyed and impatient. Mr. Tall, Dark and Pissed Off didn't look helpful, and she really didn't want to tell this stranger why she needed to get the authorities out to her farm. *I think my husband might have buried a body out back....* No. Not saying that.

"Never mind," she finished. "I hope you enjoy the house. You know what they say about Haven— it's just one letter short of Heaven." She gave him a polite smile that he didn't return. Jerk. She still didn't like him leaving, though.

She let the screen door shut. Alone again, just her and the dead body out back. The man turned to step off the porch.

Did it really matter if she contacted the police today? Her phone would be back, eventually. Or her truck would.

The skull and whatever else that went along with it in the garden wasn't going anywhere…. Not that this was a particularly comforting thought. She was just going to have to be a grown-up about the situation. She didn't need a man to take care of her, or so she'd decided. That meant handling anything that came her way.

Another huge gust swept down the mountain hollow and a crack tore the air, followed by a loud smack. And she realized Mr. Tall, Dark and Pissed Off wasn't going anywhere, either.

Not unless he was Superman and could pick an entire oak tree off his very expensive and probably very totalled car.

Chapter 2

He couldn't believe his eyes. The car was going to be a complete loss.

Sort of like his day so far. And most of the past several months.

Jake Malloy tore his stunned gaze from the mangled vehicle and glanced back at the woman banging out the doorway of the farmhouse in that eye-popping yellow T-shirt of hers. Shoulder-length gold hair framed her suddenly pale face, making her milk-chocolate eyes stand out all the more.

She was sexy as hell and she'd been annoying

him since the first time he'd talked to her on the phone last week about the rental. She asked too many questions—then and now. And he wasn't interested in providing any answers no matter how sexy she might be.

"Oh, my God," she gasped. "Your beautiful car! I'm so sorry!"

"Stop apologizing. You're not in charge of the wind, you know."

He sounded cold and rude, he knew. He was too filled with anger, too much negative emotion, for social niceties, that was all. Not too long ago, he'd had a successful career in the Charleston P.D. and he'd been a pretty decent guy. Then one fateful case had blown his life to hell and he'd spiraled into a black hole he was just beginning to dig his way out of. Supposedly, a little R&R was going to help.

"It's not your fault." He kept his voice ruthlessly hard as he went on. All he wanted now was to get the hell out of there and back to town. He moved, causing her to drop her hand from his arm, and turned to step off the porch. "I'll see if I can get my cell phone out of there and—"

"Cells don't work here. No signal."

He swore under his breath and wheeled back. She

was staring at him, her pretty face and clear eyes looking fresh and innocent, and a little wary. If Haven was one letter short of Heaven, she was an angel.

But she was no angel, no matter how sweet she looked. And Haven was turning into sheer hell and he'd only been in town an hour.

"And my truck's in the shop," she reminded him.

"Where's the closest neighbor?"

"A mile that way." She nodded in one direction. "A mile and a half the other way." She indicated the other direction.

Rain poured in sheets. Wind blasted down the damn hollow, rattling leaves and jangling chimes hanging from one end of the porch. The warmer temperatures from earlier in the day were dipping quickly.

"And when it rains like this, the low water bridge flash floods," she added. "It's very dangerous, even if you wanted to get yourself soaked hiking off to find someone who would give you a lift. It wouldn't be smart to try it. The water rises fast, faster than people expect sometimes."

She looked fragile and worried suddenly. A little bit haunted. Generally, he was good at sizing people up. Decoding body language—every movement, every look and expression—was his business, which was also why he knew that the clues could be unreliable as hell. People smiled for all sorts of reasons and happiness was only one of them, and pathological liars could lie with flawless eye contact. The more information that could be gathered, the more likely the decoding would be accurate.

His instincts had him wondering what had brought that pained expression to Keely Schiffer's face, but he reminded himself that he didn't need to know and pushed the question aside.

Looking away from her, he stared out at the wild weather for a heavy beat. He didn't really give a rat's ass about the car other than its function as transportation. It used to be important to him, his pet, his baby, and he'd invested a ridiculous amount of his modest income in it. It didn't seem important now. But he did care about being stuck out here in the middle of nowhere, and for God knew how long. Another one of life's fun twists....

Jake breathed deeply, summoning the strength and willpower to push back his own pain and control the razor-sharp edge of his temper. She didn't deserve to bear the brunt of emotions that weren't her responsibility, though he had to wonder why the hell anyone lived out here in the sticks. He was a city boy, born and bred. This little trek to

Haven hadn't been his idea, but he'd do anything, *anything*, to get his life back.

He looked back to find her still staring at him.

"If it doesn't keep up like this too long, the creek'll go down in a few hours," she said. "Dickie—he's the mechanic—will be back with my truck then, or the phones'll come back on. Or we can find you a ride."

She was talking as if this was her problem, too. For some reason, that stabbed him with a slice of hot hurt.

Wind blew a piece of her sunshine hair in her face. She brushed it out of the way, tucked it behind her ear. He could almost feel the small, soft curve of the shell of her ear beneath his fingertips…. And those eyes of hers. They were compelling, private yet vulnerable.

He forcibly reminded himself that he wasn't interested. Period.

But he wasn't getting away that easily. Not yet.

She waved him into the house. "Come on. Come inside. It's getting cold out here, and you're going to get wet. Wetter," she corrected.

He was already plenty wet, but she was right about one thing. Rain was blowing sideways onto the porch. And was he imagining it or was there something beseeching about her expression? As if

she wanted him there. Almost as if she was relieved that he was stuck there for some reason.

She was hard to read, even for him, and that was
bugging him.

"I'm a complete stranger. You don't know me
from Adam." He had the stupid urge to tell her not
to trust people. At all. Ever. He could go inside her
house, and do anything he wanted to her after that.
Not that he would. But a woman like her, alone out
in this godforsaken countryside, shouldn't be asking strange men into her home. She seemed…nice.
Genuinely nice, even if slightly annoying and
nosy.

He felt an unexpected and uncomfortable sense
of protectiveness toward her that he fought to
shake off. It wasn't his concern if she was hopelessly naive about human nature.

"You don't look like a serial killer," she said flip-
pantly, even as her sweet chocolate eyes studied him.
"You're not in the big city now. You're in Haven.
We're friendly here." She shrugged. "The people at
the store sent you over here. You're not going to hurt
me unless you're stupid. You're not stupid, are you?
Anything happens to me today, my friends'll be
looking for you, not to mention my family. Especially with your car sitting right out front."

His car that wasn't going anywhere. She had a point, but it was unrelated to why he really didn't want to go inside her house.

"I'll fix you something to drink," she said cheerily. "I owe you anyway for all the trouble of driving out here to get the keys, and if you hadn't had to do that, you wouldn't be stuck out here now with a tree trunk on top of your car."

She was already walking into the house, leaving the screen door to bang behind her and the front door open. Her slim, sexy figure disappeared through the shadowed parlor even as she kept talking, seeming to simply expect him to follow. He opened the screen door and stepped inside in spite of himself.

"You want water or tea?" she called back to him. "Or I've got some Coke."

He walked through the front room, a parlor with a slanted, scuffed hardwood floor. Rows of antique-looking photographs filled the room, solemn-faced eyes following him from the walls. The house smelled good, like cinnamon and sugar. Homey. Not that it was anything like the home he'd grown up in on the seedier streets of Charleston. Homey like…you saw on *The Andy Griffith Show*. He half expected to find Aunt Bea in the kitchen, pulling fresh-baked coffee cake out of the oven.

He arrived in the open doorframe between the kitchen and the parlor. She'd gotten down an amber-colored glass from a cabinet and was pulling every beverage known to man out of the fridge. Coke, iced tea, lemonade, milk… She'd probably offer him a cookie next.

And she was still talking.

"I've got sweet tea made, but if you don't like sweet, I can make some unsweetened. I don't mind."

"I'll just take some water." He didn't really care, truth be told. The whole scene suddenly felt terribly domestic. When was the last time he'd been in a kitchen with an attractive woman?

He didn't want to remember, but of course he could. Sheila had lived with him for two years in their nice, newly-constructed, cookie-cutter condo in South Charleston. She'd wanted to get married. He'd been in no hurry. Maybe he'd known all along it wasn't going to work out.

Sheila hadn't wasted any time when things had gone bad. Sooner was better than later, he figured. He and Sheila would have never made it anyway. She'd just been…convenient, for a while. He'd scarcely looked at a woman since. He liked being alone, detached.

And yet he found himself watching Keely

Schiffer with a sort of odd and uneasy longing. Ghost pain, he thought wryly, like a patient who felt sensation in an amputated limb. He didn't think he missed Sheila, or her constant pressure.

He hadn't realized till now that he'd been missing anything at all other than work.

"Please sit down," she said when she finally gave him the glass. "Well, I hate to say it, but this rain is a good thing because we've had an awfully dry spring. I'm just so sorry about your car. Some welcome to Haven for you, huh?"

She pulled out a chair when he didn't. He scooted it around a pile of broken pottery he noticed on the floor as he sat. He placed the glass on the table.

"I was just about to clean that up." She disappeared for a minute into the next room then came back with a broom and dustpan. She bent down, picked something up, and he saw what he'd missed at first—some sort of small package. It was wrapped in silver foil and he read the label.

"Somebody's birthday?" There, his contribution to chitchat.

"Mine."

She glanced up from sweeping the shattered bits of cream and blue pottery. Her eyes looked huge in her slender face, and as he watched, she chewed on her full, unpainted lip. He looked away from her, to the box. *Happy Birthday, Baby*. She had a gift from somebody who called her *Baby*.

He carefully returnèd his gaze to Keely. "It's your birthday today?" he asked, and told himself he was not going to look or even think about her nibble-on-me lips. Maybe she was married. He didn't know why he'd assumed she lived way out here in the sticks alone. It didn't matter to him anyway.

"Tomorrow. The present was inside the cookie jar. It fell down off the shelf." She waved her hand vaguely toward the ledge over the cabinets. It was full of decorative glass items and various pieces of pottery. "I guess he was hiding it there. My husband, I mean. A branch must have hit the roof. I guess the jar was too close to the edge of the shelf. The house really shook and—" She stood, the pottery bits tidily swept into the dustpan in one hand. "I forgot. I need to get up in the attic and check it out. If rain's coming in, I'm in real trouble."

So she *was* married.

"You'll be in trouble when your husband finds out you stumbled onto his surprise." He was feeling suddenly much lighter, more in control.

She propped the broom in the corner of the kitchen and dumped the shards of pottery in the trash before replying. "He's not going to find out. He's dead. And he left me plenty of surprises. Most of them weren't good."

The look she gave him was flat and emotionless, then a shadow slid across her expression. She looked away quickly, as if afraid he had some kind of laser vision that would see something she didn't want him to see. Jake felt more uneasy than ever, and he wasn't certain if it was because she wasn't married after all or because he wanted to know what her deceased husband had done to hurt her, and he shouldn't want to know anything about her at all.

The muted patter of raindrops on the roof filled the kitchen. The storm was slowing down. Or at least, the rain was slowing down. Wind gusted against the house, strong as ever. The clapboard farmhouse creaked a bit in the storm.

"I'm sorry," he said.

She shook her head. "No, I am. I shouldn't have said that. You shouldn't speak ill of the dead." She grabbed the wrapped box off the table and turned away, pulled open a wide kitchen drawer, shoved it inside and slammed the drawer shut.

He heard a noise like thunder and suddenly the house shook so hard, he felt the floor move under his feet. The drawers in the kitchen banged open and Keely stumbled on her feet. Automatically, he shot up, grabbing hold of her upper arms. Glass hit the floor around them from the shelves over the cabinets. He heard pictures fall in the parlor.

"Oh, God, I knew I should have had that maple tree taken down." She sounded panicked. "It's too close to the house."

"I don't think that was a tree." He hadn't heard anything strike the roof.

There was no sound for a long beat, as if even the wind held its breath, and then came a roar. The house seemed to roll under them in waves. Jake fell against the table, still holding Keely, and together they crashed onto the floor. The sting of glass cut into his back. He could feel her breasts against his chest, her quivering belly and thighs, her breaths coming in shocky pants near his cheek. He stroked his hand down her spine, only meaning to soothe. She was soft—

The floor rocked violently beneath them. "We have to get out of the house," he grunted, pulling her up with him, both of them staggering as if they'd been transported to the deck of a storm-tossed ship.

At the same time he realized the roof was coming down over them, the floorboards beneath them ripped apart and all he knew were eerie flashes of blinding red light, then plunging darkness.

Chapter 3

Darkness closed in on her with terrifying completeness. Keely heard the boom of her heartbeat, the harsh sound of her breaths, in the sudden, awful quiet. Oh, God, oh, God. She waited for the rest of the kitchen, the rest of her *house*, to fall down on top of her.

Something shifted overhead, and crashed a foot away. She nearly jumped out of her skin.

Arms she hadn't realized were holding her tightened, as if ready to shield her from anything. She couldn't see a thing, not even the man she was clinging to. Fingers reached up, touched her face. She was on top of him, she realized. They'd hit hard, him protecting her with his body.

"Are you all right?" He was little more than a deep, disembodied voice in the terrible blackness.

"I think so." Her voice wobbled. Was the world still shaking? She bit her lip to keep from hyperventilating.

Jake Malloy grunted in pain, and she scrambled off him, pulling him up with her till they sat on debris. She could feel nothing but debris surrounding them.

"Where are we?" he asked her. "We fell into some kind of basement. Is this a cellar?"

She nodded, swallowed thickly, realizing then he couldn't see her.

"Yes. It's the cellar." Her head reeled. The kitchen ceiling had started coming down and the floor had opened up. The cold dampness of the cellar seeped through her then and she shivered. Shock. Maybe she was in shock. The cellar was low-ceilinged. They'd only dropped maybe seven feet.

And the ceiling boards from the kitchen must have covered the gap in the floor above. She felt as if her heart might pound out of her chest.

"There's a door, over here." She pushed to her feet,

stumbling slightly on the uneven piles of wreckage she couldn't see. "The ground slopes down this way and the cellar's reached by a door below the rear of the house." In the thick darkness, she felt him reach for her hand. His hold felt strong and warm on hers. Oddly safe. Together, they took baby steps across the debris, guided only by her sense of direction, which was, at the moment, rocky.

She reached out with her hand, feeling her way. Her fingers brushed against the rough, peeling paint of the wooden door to the cellar. She pulled her other hand from his, heart thumping as she grabbed the handle. Debris in the cellar made opening the door nearly impossible.

"Wait."

She could feel the brush of Jake beside her, hear the sound of broken boards being tossed out of the way.

"Try now," he said.

The door creaked as she pulled it inward, still scraping across smaller bits of rubble. She pushed around it, reaching forward into the pitch-black. And stopping short at the sensation of rough, jagged material blocking the way.

No, no, no. There had been no light around the door, it hit her suddenly. No light not because it was dark outside but because part of the house must have fallen this way!

And who knew how much weight there was in wreckage blocking them from climbing back up into the kitchen. "We're trapped," she whispered in horror.

"We'll be all right. We'll get out of here."

He sounded so sure of himself, she almost believed him for a minute.

She swallowed hard. "How?"

"Rescue workers will be coming—"

"Do you know how long it will take them to get here, this far out of town?" If they even could. They'd have to wait to even try if the low water bridge was flooded. What was happening in the town? What about her store? What about her *house*? It was gone, clearly gone. And yet she still found that impossible to grasp. She loved her house in all its faded glory, from its American gothic farmhouse architecture to its walls teeming with family history. "Gemini" tea roses were her grandmother's favorite, that's why she was planting more of that specific variety. She was supposed to be planting roses right now. A normal day, planting roses, waiting for her truck to be done at the shop. She'd have fixed herself a sandwich for dinner, maybe a bowl of

soup, and watched the news, followed by the latest
season of her favorite amateur singing competition, and the new medical drama. She'd have gone
to bed in her antique spool feather bed covered by
a hand-sewn block quilt and read a magazine till she
went to sleep.

Her life was boring, maybe, but she liked it. It
was quiet and sensible.

Nothing made sense right now, especially how
much she didn't want this stranger to let go of her.
She clutched blindly at his shirt as she felt him turn.

"Are you all right?" he asked. "Did you cut
yourself on anything?"

She felt his hands moving down her shoulders,
her arms, as if checking. "No. I mean, yes. I'm all
right. What happened? What could do this to my
house?" She could barely stretch her mind around
the horrifying reality of it. "Oh, God. That was—"

"An earthquake."

We don't have earthquakes in West Virginia.
She hadn't realized she'd said that out loud till he
answered her.

"Not very often. But if we weren't just at the
epicenter of that one, I don't know what it was."

Her mind stumbled from the realization. That
first time she'd felt the house shake and the cookie

jar had fallen off the shelf had just been a precursor of what was coming.

There had been no tree hitting the roof at all.

"My house—"

One hundred years old, and it was in pieces over her head. Everything that had been in her family for generations— Her parents, Howard and Roxie Bennett, preferred their spacious home with all the modern conveniences and close to town. Her older sister and two brothers already had their own homes, too, by the time Granny Opal had died. Keely and Ray had needed a place, and so the farmhouse had gone to Keely, who had gladly accepted it. But now... What was she going to do without a house?

Another thought struck her. "What was that red light? Did you see it? Oh, my God. Was that fire?" No, it couldn't have been fire. They'd know if the house was on fire above them. So what—

"I don't know. Probably electricity snapping, who knows. Forget your house." A beat stretched, taut. "I'm sorry," he added, gentler. The unexpected kindness in his touch and voice sent her into a panic. She'd been hesitant to so much as ask him for a favor not too many minutes ago. Now she wanted to climb up his powerful, hard body and beg him not to leave her for a second in this pitch-black nightmare. He was the only other human being in her world, her touchstone to reality.

"You're okay, and that's all that matters," he continued. "Come on. You can worry about your house later."

As if he sensed she was an inch away from royally flipping out, he stroked his hands up and down her arms again. His touch was warm and strong and she didn't want him to stop. Probably, he didn't want to deal with a hysterical woman. He hadn't seemed this kind and patient earlier.

She was on fear overload, and she hated that. She was used to taking care of herself by now. She didn't need anyone, especially not a man. *Get it together.*

"I'm okay," she repeated back to him. The aching of her bones hit her, surfacing through the adrenaline. She was lucky she hadn't broken anything in the fall, even as short as it had been. Lucky he hadn't broken anything, either.

"You're okay, too, right?" she asked, to be sure.

"I'm fine. Tell me what's in here. Do you keep a flashlight somewhere?" He sounded steady, composed, organized.

"No such luck. But matches—maybe." She worked to catalog the cellar in her mind, recall what was where. She had to be strong now. Not fall apart.

One wall of the cellar had been lined with glass canning jars. Some empty now, others still packed with the fruits of last summer's gardening. Some old wooden stools. Boxes and antique trunks filled with forgotten items that had worked their way out of the farmhouse at one time or another. Tools that hadn't been used in ages. A couple of old tables. Basically, junk. The cellar was full of junk. The wall on the other side was storage. There were some candles somewhere, stashed on one of those over-packed shelves....

Vanilla-scented. They'd been a gift from a Christmas exchange party at church last year. She hated vanilla candles and she'd stuck them in the cellar, not able to bring herself to just throw them out. If they were still here...

She'd absolutely love, adore and worship the scent of vanilla right now.

Hadn't she left an old box of matches here somewhere? And a can of gasoline. She'd used the matches and gas to burn the brush pile last summer.

"This way." She moved along the wall to the

right of the door. Away from the center of the cellar, there was less debris from above, but there was shattered glass everywhere. She walked carefully, but stumbled anyway when something creaked overhead.

Jake caught her as she made a strangled cry and she found herself dragged up against that hard, powerful body of his.

"Whoa." He held her for a long beat.

She couldn't see him, not even his eyes and they had to be only inches away. He smelled good. She hadn't noticed before, but she did now. He smelled *really* good. Woodsy and male. She was ready to cling on to him like he was some kind of life preserver. He definitely exuded some kind of raw masculine energy that was messing with her mind, which was hardly stable as it was. Her head was all over the place, reeling.

"Careful," he murmured.

"I'm trying." She'd better try harder.

The air in the cellar was suddenly thick with an odd tension. They were practically buried alive down here. He could be the last human being on earth she'd ever know. She was scared, terrified really, of dying before they were rescued. She'd lost her house, maybe her business for all she knew.

But in the face of losing her life, suddenly it didn't amount to much.

Her family and friends— She had no idea what had happened to them. All she could do was desperately hope and pray. Images of her parents, her friends, flashed like photos in a slideshow in her mind.

A sob choked her throat and she swallowed it down. She couldn't do anything for anyone now but herself and this stranger beside her. She didn't realize she was crying till she felt something wet and cold trickle down her cheek.

"Hey. Come on. Let's find those matches."

She nodded, then tried to find her voice.

"Okay." She squeezed her eyes shut, struggling to stop the tears.

A hand touched her face. Jake Malloy's hand.

"Aww, now," he said, softer now, brushing at the tear.

Instinctively, she curled her arms around him, her hands sliding under his jacket, letting him pull her tight and comfort her there in that black void under her ruined house. She didn't understand how she could trust him like this, but it didn't matter. His arms wiped out that horrific fear.

Her head rested against his chest and she could

hear his heartbeat, steady and sure as hers was not. He kept right on being rock solid even with the world falling apart around them.

And in the back of her mind, a crazy thought entered. She wondered what it would be like to kiss him. He moved against her, just slightly, as if checking his balance, and she shook herself and started to pull back.

Something cold and hard stuck out of the waistband of his jeans, beneath the cover of his jacket, as she drew her hands down and away. Something cold and hard and metal…

Her heart stopped and total fear slammed back in on her. She felt him freeze, and she moved quickly before he could, grabbed it in one hand and stumbled back, knowing what she held. Not needing any light.

She was holding a gun.

Chapter 4

He felt the cold metal slide away from the waist-band of his jeans and before he could move, she was gone, nothing but a ragged gasp in the darkness. He lunged forward then stopped cold at the low, fearful, shaking sound of her voice.

"Don't come near me. I'll shoot."

"No, you won't." He hoped she wouldn't. Hell, he didn't know. He didn't move.

He could feel his heart thumping hard against his ribs. And he could have sworn he could hear hers, thumping, too. She was scared and he didn't blame her, but he needed to get back in control of the situation. Scaring her more wasn't the way.

"I know how to use a gun," she said, that soft, low voice of hers still uneven. "What I don't know is what you're doing with one."

"It's licensed," he told her, keeping his voice steady, reassuring. "I have a right to carry it. There's no need to be afraid."

"I'm trapped here with you and a gun. I think I can decide for myself if I should be afraid or not."

"You already pointed out that everyone in town knows I'm here. My car is still outside. Rescuers will get here eventually. Why would I want them to find me here, in a cellar with a dead body and my gun? I'm not going to shoot you. I'm not stupid, remember?" Reason, he had to use reason on her. She was already frightened, for good cause, by the quake and the destruction of her house and their desperate situation.

She was silent for a beat and he could hear the house creak over them again. She could hear it, too, and he heard her feet shift on the rubble, knew she was unnerved even more, wondered if she was trying to decide whether she needed to hold his gun, or hold him, to feel most safe.

"Do you think I want to spend God knows how

many hours alone down here, waiting for help, with a dead body?" he asked quietly. "I don't want to shoot you, Keely. I—"

His throat closed up a bit and the next words were hard to admit, but he had to make a choice, too. Risk a little of himself, or risk his life if he let a very frightened woman continue to point a gun at him. Situations got out of hand sometimes. He knew that too well.

"I like you," he finished finally. "Why would I want to shoot you?"

She didn't say anything for long seconds. He felt the electric pull of her even through the dark. She was thinking, he knew. Thinking about whether she could trust him or not.

It appeared she wasn't so naive, after all.

"You walked up to my door with a gun," she said. "And I want to know why." Her voice strengthened.

She was pulling herself together. That hadn't taken long, and it occurred to him that she had a tough spine inside that very sweet, hot, bombshell-quality body of hers.

He *did* like her, he realized with a shock, even though she had annoyed him quite a bit, from the first time he'd spoken with her on the phone about the rental, with questions he didn't want to answer.

He liked her in spite of himself because she was nice. Even when he was rude to her, she was nice. In fact, she was too nice. Too nice for him. His instinct to get away from her as quickly as possible had been a good one.

Now he *couldn't* get away from her and she was going to take her opportunity to ask questions again, and he was going to have to give her answers whether he liked it or not. And he didn't like it at all.

"I'm a cop."

The house lay so still around them, he could hear the very low intake of her breath, sense the tension emanating from her body as his words sunk in. His gut tightened, waiting for her to respond.

"A *cop*?" She didn't sound like she really believed him.

He figured she'd thought he operated on the opposite side of the law, based on his appearance. He'd worked undercover most of the past few years and his wardrobe had suffered in keeping with his cases. Not that he cared or that it mattered. He was supposed to be resting and relaxing, not dressing for success.

In truth, he was just biding his time. He didn't need rest and relaxation. He needed to get back to work. The damn thing was, the chief wouldn't let him. The department shrink had said he wasn't dealing with his grief. Go to the country, the chief had ordered. Get some perspective. Unwind. One month. Then he'd let him come back to work. He'd suggested Haven. The chief had grown up here.

Jake had thought he was dealing with his grief just fine. How the hell was someone supposed to take it when they were responsible for their partner getting blown up right in front of them? And people had called him a hero. He'd just wanted to get back to work. He *still* wanted to get back to work. He wanted to *bury* himself in work. No thinking. No feeling. And certainly no consorting with the locals. He didn't want any entanglements.

But here he was in Haven, trapped in a cellar with a beautiful woman. How had that happened?

"Charleston Police Department," he told her.

"And I'm supposed to know that's the truth how…?" she asked.

"Because I'm telling you it's the truth…." he said. "I'm one of the good guys, Keely. I promise." He waited a beat. "If you don't mind, I don't really like it when people point guns at me," he said. "It makes me worry about whether I'm going to get to keep breathing. You stop pointing the gun at me and we find a candle, then I'll show you my badge and ID. Deal?"

He heard the soft click of the chamber pushing open.

"I'm going to take the bullets out. You don't mind, do you?" she asked.

"Not at all."

She hadn't lied about knowing how to operate a weapon. And she might believe him—or might not—but she wasn't going to leave the gun loaded. Again, not so naive, after all.

It wouldn't do her a whole lot of good if he wanted to wrestle the empty gun away from her and find the bullets, but it would buy her time. Better, he supposed she was figuring, than letting him wrestle the gun away from her loaded.

She'd probably just put the bullets in her back pocket. There weren't a whole lot of other options available.

He heard the gun drop on the debris behind her.

"I know you can pick it up," she said then. "I know you can get the bullets away from me. But," she added dryly, "I suppose you're right. You're pretty stuck if help comes and I'm laying here in a pool of blood. Wouldn't be too smart on your part. I just don't like loaded guns, so let's not keep it that way. Okay?" She still wasn't completely trusting him.

"Okay."

Tentative truce. Fragile, very fragile, he'd guess. He'd take it.

"They'd know you did it," she added.

"Yes."

"You'd go to prison."

"Definitely."

"For the rest of your life."

"Probably."

"Or get the death sentence."

"There's no death sentence in West Virginia."

She was silent for a long beat. Disappointed, probably.

"You know what they do to guys like you in prison," she said finally.

In spite of himself, he felt a slow lift to his mouth. He actually almost laughed.

"Are you saying I'm cute?" What the hell was he doing now? *Flirting* with her?

He heard her blow out an irritated breath. Yeah, she thought he was cute. She probably hadn't meant to give that away.

"I'm not saying you're cute," she said tensely.

"I'm not saying you're anything but on your way to the slammer if you try to hurt me."

He reminded himself that it wasn't important what she thought of him as long as she stopped holding a gun on him.

Sobering, he said, "I'm not going to shoot you, Keely. I don't want to hurt you in any way."

She was silent for another long stretch.

"I'd probably never find the candles and matches without you," he tacked on. "Plus, I'd be lonely down here waiting for help."

"Oh, yeah."

He heard her move, slowly, carefully, toward one wall of the cellar. Good. Back to business.

"There's a trunk over here, somewhere," she said.

He followed the sound of her voice and her footsteps. She'd knelt, was clearing debris from something. He went to work with her, removing boards and bits of plaster and who knew what else.

"This is it," she said, and her voice rose, confident, hopeful. The trunk lid creaked open and she fumbled around inside. "Here they are."

The box opened with a soft sound then she struck a long match, held it up.

She wasn't just a voice in the dark anymore. Her eyes glowed in the light from the flame, wary and still scared. He knelt there, close to her, close enough to fill his nostrils with her heady scent, feel overpowered for a second by the vulnerable look on her face.

Apple. She smelled like apple. Deliciously sweet.

He reached for his wallet, flipped out his ID and badge for her to see.

"You don't have to be scared of me," he said quietly, tucking the truth of his identity back in his pocket. "I really don't want to hurt you, Keely. I'm not going to. I promise."

She stared at him, and time locked, forever, it seemed, then she blinked and turned her gaze down, away from him.

"I don't believe in promises," she said so softly, it was nearly a whisper. "People lie all the time. So cut it out with the promises. I'm not interested."

The heart he wasn't supposed to feel tightened a little at the break in her voice. She'd been hurt, badly, he had no doubt now. Probably by that dead husband of hers.

But he wasn't responsible. It bothered him, anyway. That look in her eyes, that pain in her thready voice, *bothered* him. This was more than police instinct to read and study people. This was about her. And that wasn't good.

"I'm sorry anyone ever lied to you," he said, and it was too late to bite the words back even if he really wanted to.

She glanced back up and he saw emotion shining in her eyes. She cleared her throat, blinked back tears. "There are candles over there somewhere."

The long match was half-burned when she stood, moved to the other wall. Broken canning jars lay everywhere and she crouched again, searching. He went after her.

"Here they are." The joy in her voice was catching. "We have light!" She stuck one of the thick candles inside one of the intact jars and lit it with the match, then stood. The scent of warm vanilla rose around her, mixing with the ripe apple scent. She smelled good enough to eat and his libido was taking his brain in directions he didn't want to go.

He stood in front of her when she turned, the candle in the jar in her hand. He wanted to kiss her. Her mouth was right there, inches away. It was crazy, ridiculous. Her hair fell around her face in shimmery strands, like spun gold, wildly sexy and just begging for a man to tangle his fingers into it, pull her face close and— The strength of his very vivid fantasy shocked him and left him with a weird, edgy feeling as he reminded himself that he wasn't interested in any kind of relationship, with Keely Schiffer or anyone else.

"We're going to be okay, right?" she said then.

"Help will come. Your friends and your family will make sure of that." And he was sure she had friends and family that cared about her. He could just tell. She was all apple pie goodness through and through. A nice, wholesome country girl.

She couldn't have been more foreign to his experience if she'd hailed from another continent. Maybe that was the trouble. He was used to women who wielded their sexuality like a weapon. She was innocently sensual, naively seductive. She was killing him.

"If they're even okay." She bit her lip and he could hear the fear in her voice. "I don't know if they're okay."

"Faith," he offered. "You have to go on faith for now." He didn't know where that came from. He hadn't had much faith lately. He wanted her to have it, though. "We were lucky, you know? We may be trapped here, but we're all right. They were lucky, too. Just believe that for now. There's nothing else you can do."

He smoothed the hair back from her face even when he knew he shouldn't touch her more than necessary. He couldn't seem to *stop* touching her, but he forced himself to. He dropped his hand back to his side.

What the hell was wrong with him?

"You're right, I know," she whispered, her eyes holding him. "Stop being so nice," she said suddenly. "It's freaking me out."

He laughed, surprised by her remark, and loved it when she smiled through the shine of tears in her gaze. It was an unexpectedly satisfying reward.

"Sorry. I can go back to being an asshole if you want."

She laughed now. "No, I guess I don't want you to do that. I'm stuck with you here, after all." She cocked her head, studied him. "We're stuck with each other."

He nodded. "Looks that way."

"For who knows how long," she added. Her gaze moved, swept the cellar. In the flickering candlelight, the wreckage was stunning. "What now?"

Chapter 5

Keely knew what she wanted to do. Run away. Jake Malloy, Mr. Tall, Dark and Pissed-Off, was more complicated than she'd expected. He made her feel safe at the same time he made her want to run away screaming.

There was no place to run, though, so she was going to have to trust him. He was a *cop*. Not a thug, a cop. A hot, delectable, adorable cop and here she was, trapped with him.

"We could keep standing here," he said, too

close, way too close to her, looking dangerously sexy. "But that might get old."

Thank God he wasn't touching her anymore. She liked it too much when he touched her. She'd already made the big mistake of letting him hold her. Bad, Keely.

She'd be better off if she didn't remember how good that had felt.

"If we clean some of this up, there are some old tables here. We could sit on them, or stretch out on them to sleep. We could be here for a long time." She shivered, thinking of how long it could be. "We could be here for days."

"We won't be. Come on."

He set to work, and she was more than ready to occupy herself with something, anything, that would take her mind off the situation—the way they were trapped, and the heat she thought she saw simmering in Jake Malloy's eyes. Heat for her. It could be her too-vivid imagination, but she didn't think so, and as they worked, carefully moving the heavier debris, she worked, too, on stomping out any thoughts about it.

The past was always there, reminding her that a man in her life wasn't what she needed. She'd given herself way too easily to Ray. The sex had been okay, and she missed that, but it was the way he'd taken over her life that had really hurt.

She was a sucker, but no more. Ray had cheated on her, stolen from her, lied to her. No more trusting men, not further than she could throw them. *She wanted to throw Jake to the floor and throw herself after him.* Oh, God, where had that thought come from?

"So why are you in Haven anyway?" she asked as they worked together. "I thought you said you were here on business. Are you here on a case? Undercover?" He looked like a man who lived for danger.

"I'm here on some R & R."

"Why Haven?"

He shrugged. "My chief recommended it. He's from around here. Jerry Overton."

"Oh, I know the Overtons," Keely said.

"Guess everyone knows just about everyone around here."

"Yeah. Pretty much. Small town. It's nice, though. Well, most of the time. People care. Are you from Charleston?"

She was just making conversation, passing time. She wasn't trying to get to know him better. No, not her.

"Grew up there. Born and bred. City boy."

"You'll love Haven. It's—"

"Friendly. One letter short of heaven. Uh-huh."

He didn't sound like he planned on loving Haven. "How long are you staying?" He'd put down a month's rent, that's all she knew.

"Just the month. Then I'm headed back to work. Back to the city."

Back to city lights and cell phone service, she guessed. He wouldn't be around long. Good thing she wasn't going to get attached to him.

They had a couple of tables cleared and pushed together, and with the jarred light on a nearby shelf, Keely dragged a couple of quilts out of the trunk and climbed up on one. She wrapped one of the quilts around herself, pulling her knees to her chest. It was getting colder. The cellar was always cold, but night had to be coming on and temperatures dipped hard in Appalachia even at this time of year once the sun went down.

Jake took the other blanket and did the same. His gaze caught hers with unflinching gravity. He'd said they'd be rescued soon, as if he had no doubt, but she didn't believe him. No telling how long they could be stuck down here.

"Are you hungry?" she asked. "There's food."

They weren't going to starve, at least. Not all the canned goods had broken. There were green beans, jams, apples, pears, relishes…. Not exactly a square meal, but this wasn't a situation that called for being a picky eater.

"Not now. Did you can this stuff?"

She nodded. "I always grow a big garden."

"Gardening, canning, handling guns… You're a real all-around woman."

He was looking at her, and she felt herself blush. The candle was behind her, leaving her face in shadow, so she hoped he couldn't tell.

"I'm a country girl," she said.

"I noticed."

She wondered what he meant by that. Maybe he thought she was a hillbilly hick. Like she cared.

"We could try to get some sleep, I guess," she suggested.

"I don't sleep much lately," he said.

"You lie awake, stressing?" She did that, too.

"Sometimes."

He sounded guarded, as if he didn't want to admit to any vulnerability. She felt another twinge of something, a disquieting bonding with him that she never would have expected. She wondered why he was on R & R.

"I've had trouble getting used to sleeping alone," she admitted. "I don't miss much about Ray, but I miss that. Having someone there to hold me." She pulled the quilt tighter, felt the guilt hit her. "I shouldn't say that."

"Why not?" Jake asked quietly. "If it's how you feel, say it. It's not like Ray is going to hear it and be offended."

That almost made her laugh, but it was too sad. Even if she didn't miss much about their marriage, he'd been too young to die. He'd loved her in his way, hadn't he? He'd bought her a birthday present six months in advance. That had to say something. She'd probably never find that little box in the rubble that was left of her house now, but it was the thought that counted.

Of course, he may have left a dead body in her rose bed, too.

"I'm never getting married again," she said. He watched her, steady, and she had the weird sensation that they were the only two people left on Earth. Down here, trapped in the cellar, they might as well be. The flicker of the candle played light and shadow on the hard planes of his face, softening them. "You ever been married?"

Did he miss having someone to hold him at night?

He shook his head. "Never. Got close once, but I escaped."

"How?"

"She dumped me."

He was so matter-of-fact, she couldn't tell if he was upset about it or not.

"Do you miss her?"

A beat passed before he answered. "No. Now that sounds bad, doesn't it?"

"Dating anyone?"

"No." His smile was heart-stoppingly slow. "Why? Want to set me up?"

She laughed. "No!" Selfishly, no. But that wasn't something she needed to be thinking about, wanting him for herself. Even if she was more aware of him right now than she'd ever been aware of a man before in her entire life.

This conversation wasn't going anywhere good. She was starting to feel…hot. Maybe she was displacing her fears about the situation. But that was no excuse for being stupid. She didn't know Jake, not at all. Her first impression of him had been that he was angry and impatient. Then he'd seemed possibly dangerous. Now she didn't know what to think.

Other than that he was single and available, and she didn't need to be thinking about that.

"Wow," he finally said. "That was pretty certain." His lips curved further, proving he wasn't offended.

"It's none of my business. I shouldn't have asked." She sounded prim enough now, didn't she? "And I don't set people up anyway, so it's not personal."

"It's okay," he said. "I'm not interested in dating."

"Planning to be a monk?"

Jeez, what had made her ask *that*? She felt her face heat again, dammit. She was embarrassing herself.

"No, not exactly," he said, amusement tinging his voice. Then he seemed to sober. "Men and women, they make things too complicated, you know? Defining and analyzing what should be natural and easy."

"What do you mean?"

"Relationships. Sex. Marriage just gets courts and judges and lawyers involved."

If you got divorced it got courts and judges and lawyers involved. She got the idea Jake expected marriage to end in divorce…. Well, maybe if Ray had lived, that's where they would have ended up. If she'd finally gotten the courage to take the steps necessary.

"You don't believe in love?" she asked softly.

"I don't know about love," he answered. "I've

seen what happens to people who think they're in it, though. I'm not interested."

She couldn't argue with him, even when she felt a disquieting twinge at his flat words. She felt the same, didn't she?

Then she heard it. And this time she knew what it was. It wasn't thunder. It was an aftershock. The house shook over their heads. Jake wasted no time even as the breath was so stalled in Keely's throat she hadn't thought past it.

Powerful arms hurled over her, rolling her down off the table, onto the floor where his body, again, protected her and then pulled her underneath. The quilt she'd been covered in, and his arms and legs, tangled around her. Debris crashed down from above and glass jars clattered from the shelves.

Darkness fell with almost violent suddenness.

The candle was gone, and as more and more material rained down, she knew so was everything else. Everything but Jake, here, holding her so tightly. *Oh, God, oh, God.*

Silence, then another creak, and another piece of her hundred-year-old house tumbled down onto the debris already filling the cellar. She could hear her heart beating hard, feel Jake's as he held her.

"We're going to die," she whispered.

"No, we're not. We're not going to die." His voice was raspy, close. She couldn't see him, but he was here, his breath warm against her ear.

"You don't know that."

"You're right," he admitted. "I don't know that."

She shuddered and he gathered her closer. He shifted, moving the quilt so that it was all the way around both of them, his hands inside it, stroking her, comforting her.

"We're safe as we can be, here. We'll stay under this table."

The table had shielded them from what had rained down. If not for his quick action—

"I'm not going anywhere," she whispered into his throat. How many aftershocks until the house crushed the table, crushed them, trapping them under its weight? She noticed he wasn't telling her they were going to be okay anymore.

"Neither am I. I'm right here."

And he was, he was right there, his arms around her. What if he hadn't come out to the farmhouse today? She would have been here by herself.

"I'm glad you're here because I don't want to be alone," she breathed.

"You're not alone."

She turned her head slowly. She couldn't see him but that didn't matter. She could *feel* him.

Then she could feel *it* again, another aftershock on the heels of the last one. And the terror was so all-consuming, it took over and she sucked in a breath to let out with a scream—but she couldn't, he wouldn't let her, and even as the world fell down on them again, he covered her mouth with his. And she wanted it, wanted him. She wanted to think of nothing but this moment and this man because everything else was so horrific.

He was safe, he was here, he was now, and now was all she had left.

Jake told himself he had no choice, he had to kiss her. She was losing it, totally, and that wasn't going to do her, or him, any good. They had hours left, hours or days, who knew, before they were rescued. If they were rescued.

If they didn't die any minute now.

He slid his hands down the length of her, pulling her near and she all but climbed up him, quivering and desperate, kissing him back. Then she tore free, and he could feel her gaze, inches over him, her breaths coming in shocky pants.

The shaking had stopped. The blackness around

them was silent again, silent but for the pounding of her heart. Silent like a tomb.

She wasn't the only one losing it, he realized. He was, too, and what the hell difference did it make?

He leaned up, just a hair, and she leaned down and they were kissing again, hard and starving and oh, so sweet-hot. He wanted her.

Dear God, he wanted her. And given how she clung to him, kissing him back with just as much annihilating fever, she felt the same way.

She was soft, so damnably soft, and he let the taste of her take over. He pushed back the quilt, slid his hands down the denim covering her sweet little rear and up, inside her shirt, skimming the satiny heat of her skin. She let out a sound of need, ripped her mouth away from him.

"I'm scared," she whispered. "I don't want to die scared."

"I'm here. I'm right here. I promise." She needed him, and he needed a purpose. Or maybe he needed an excuse for needing *her*.

"Don't go away."

"I can't. And I don't want to." He moved one arm to reach up, touch her face, read her fear and need as if he were a blind man reading Braille. His other arm skimmed up along her spine.

She shifted, in the dark, moving beside him, where he'd pushed the quilt off of them. She lay there, breathing softly, as if waiting…. He'd moved with her, one arm wrapped over her middle where her shirt rose up, baring her flat belly.

He felt the strangest sensation. Awe. She was offering herself to him as if there were no tomorrow—because she didn't know if there was one. And if there wasn't…

Then she wanted to die in his arms.

"Jake?"

Her whispery voice wobbled just a bit.

"I'm here. I'm not going anywhere. I promised."

Keely wanted to tell him again not to make any promises, but then what did it matter now? She pulled at her shirt. She made it disappear then she was there again, beside him on the quilt.

"Keely—"

"Don't say anything," she begged softly. "Just kiss me till I can't think."

He did, he kissed her, tenderly this time, not hard, not fast, and it felt so natural and easy. His fingers swept up her torso as his tongue drove into her mouth and he swallowed the gasp of pleasure as his thumb and forefinger circled her nipple then squeezed it gently.

Her kiss turned hungry, fueling his, and his fingers slid down now, down to her pants. She ripped at his jacket, clawing at his shirt as he slid his hand inside her jeans and felt, *knew*, how much she wanted him, wanted this.

It was a bad idea, she thought suddenly. She was still thinking and she knew it was a bad idea. She didn't know him. She didn't do one-night stands.

She opened her mouth to say it was a bad idea, but she forgot why as she moved her hips against his hand, pressing that damp, pulsing part of her into his fingers. The thud of their heartbeats charged the air, interwoven with fear and hope, survival and desperation. Then her hands traveled their way back to his shoulders, pushing back his jacket, tearing at his shirt. He sat up, head down to keep from hitting the underside of the table.

Jacket—gone. Shirt—gone. Jeans…

Gone, too.

She heard him go through his pocket, the thud of what she guessed was a wallet hitting the floor. Protection. He'd remembered to think of protection while she could barely remember her name.

Then he was back, slipping his hand down her bare belly…bare thighs.

Yes. This was what she wanted. And she knew it, couldn't pretend she didn't.

His fingers slid inside her and she gripped his shoulders hard, and a moan escaped her mouth just before he covered it with his. She wrapped her arms all the way around him, tugging him down over top of her. She felt the whole length of him against her, fitting perfectly, felt blood surging low in his body. She wanted him to bury himself inside her, right now. But first he kissed her eyelids, her nose, her chin. She wanted him to kiss her everywhere.

Trembling, she cupped the back of his head, pulled him down toward her breasts as she arched up to him now. He took one nipple, then another into his mouth and she sighed and writhed under him. His response was real, heat and hunger.

He tongued down her stomach, lower, to the *V* of her thighs where he placed his mouth there, at the swollen center of her, and sucked so hard, she cried out in a sound of pain and pleasure that begged him not to stop, begged him to make her forget everything but this intense thing happening right here between them.

Mindless sex.

One harmless fantasy before she died. And since things were pretty much headed in that direction, she was allowed.

She moved, lifting her legs, draping them over his shoulders, clearly begging for more, and he gave it, circling her then sucking again, harder, not stopping even as she clawed her fingers into his hair and made short, gasping sobs. Convulsions ripped through her as he replaced his tongue with his fingers and she felt so tight inside, so hot, she thought she'd die right there if he couldn't be there, right there, with her, all of him.

"Keely—"

"Don't leave me."

"I'm not leaving. I'm here."

"Closer."

He thrust inside her. Taut contractions gripped her as he sank in over and over, and she shattered again, and whatever was left of reality, of fear, was left far behind, lost to the world they made for themselves. The friction of his heat, her own pent-up and denied need, exploded and he shuddered into her as she wrapped her arms and legs tightly around him, going up into flames right along with him—again.

In what was left of her brain, a tiny piece of her mind broke loose from the sheer bliss of physical feeling to spin the thought through her that this was something different. Sex with Ray hadn't been like this.

But like so much else in her day, that thought made no sense.

She slept curled into his shoulder, and woke by surreal degrees to a terrible roar.

Chapter 6

The roar was followed by dead silence.

She heard her name, called down through a crack in the debris above. A crack of light. That had been lifting equipment she'd heard. They were being rescued!

"I'm here! We're here!" she called back.

"Don't move," came the order back.

Jake's arm tightened around her. Jake. The stranger. The stranger she'd…

Had a mindless fantasy with before she died.

Only she wasn't going to die. And she was so happy about that, but—

Complicated emotions ricocheted through her.

There were more sounds, debris being hand-removed as they closed in on the pocket of safety she and her oh-so-familiar-now stranger had found in the cellar under her demolished farmhouse. She felt a flash of fear as one piece of debris broke free and fell, crashing onto the pile of rubble she could now clearly see beyond the shelter of the table they lay beneath.

Then she realized she was naked. Jake was naked. Oh, God. *She was going to be rescued naked.*

Unlike her, he seemed totally unembarrassed by his nakedness, simply went about fixing it in the tightness of their quarters. Cool, composed, always.

He yanked on his jeans, handing over her shirt, separating out his and hers. Without a word. What was he thinking? What had *she* been thinking? It might have been natural and easy last night, but it didn't feel natural and easy now.

Had there ever been a worse morning after in the history of one-night-stand morning-afters?

In the awkwardness of the confined space, she managed to wiggle into her clothes. She utilized her nearly nonexistent acting skills to behave as if this was normal for her.

One-night stand. She hated that term. But what else could she call it? Comfort, need, shock, fantasy. Whatever the reason, she'd had a one-night stand with someone she did not intend to have a relationship with. A stranger, no less.

The rubble of the cellar surrounded them. For one moment, it was utterly still, utterly silent from above. Then something moved.

Something moved in the cellar.

At first, it was only the sound of movement that she knew. A soft *thud, thud, thud*, like something very small, something very light.

She could feel Jake behind her, half-sitting as she was.

Then she saw it, the box. The box from Ray. End over end, tumbling toward her. Moving on its own. But it couldn't move on its own. Another aftershock, another aftershock was coming—

A scream rose in her throat.

The box rolled over a pile of broken boards and stopped, a hand's reach away.

Stopped, just stopped. Her mind reeled, panic and confusion. No aftershock. Nothing. Just the box had moved, nothing but the box. And now it had stopped.

A steel ladder dropped, settled roughly in the debris. Boots came down after.

Jake moved, nudged her back.

"Go."

She got to her knees, dressed, thank God, and ready to crawl out from under the table, toward rescue. She grabbed the box. The rescue equipment must have dislodged it. Somehow. She looked back at Jake. It was morning, had to be. Time seemed elastic, stretching back and forth in her mind from the shock of the quake to the shock of what they'd done after, and hazy from sleep and the surreal comprehension that they'd survived, after all.

In a moment of high stress, they'd shared a bond. It was over now. A mindless little fantasy.

But dammit, she wasn't a one-night-stand kind of girl and was she crazy or had that been the most explosive sex ever? Maybe it was just the emotional thing, the fear and the drama of their circumstances that had heightened her awareness. Yes, that made sense. She needed *something* to make sense.

"Are we just going to…pretend this didn't happen?" she whispered. Oh, God, what did she even want him to say?

His unreadable gaze was tight on hers. "Is that what you want?"

She didn't know what she wanted. What did *he*

want? "It was just a one-night stand. Right?" She needed him to clarify it for her. She needed him to say it then she'd be fine with it. "I mean, I've had them before. It's no big deal."

Oh, jeez, she'd just made herself sound like a slut. And it wasn't even true.

"Keely Schiffer?" The rescuer called her again.

"Go. Go find your family." Jake pushed her gently toward the light. "Everything's going to be okay."

She nodded, couldn't speak, wasn't sure what she'd say if she did. That she was so grateful that he'd been there for her in the frightening darkness? That she was embarrassed and could he possibly just forget it ever happened because that uninhibited woman who'd all but begged him to make love to her was as much of a stranger to her as he was? That she wanted to know if she'd ever see him again?

That last question was more frightening than the others combined. That grip she needed to get was troublingly elusive.

"Keely Schiffer?"

She turned to the rescue worker, his booted feet now planted firmly on the precarious debris.

"Anyone hurt?"

She shook her head.

"How many do you have down here?" the man

asked, his flashlight beaming into the dark corners of the cellar even as with his other arm he took hold of her.

"Just one other person was in the house," she answered. "Jake Malloy." Already, Jake was crawling out from beneath the table, carefully rising to a stand on the debris beside her.

Another rescuer came down the ladder, grabbed for Keely's hand, and the first rescuer handed her over. The ladder shifted as she climbed, sending ripples of remembered shock through her, fear of another quake speeding her feet.

Everything happened quickly after that. The smashed remains of her house blurred across her vision as she rose from the huge pile that was left of her house. She tried to focus on the devastation, but her head reeled at the sight of it even as powerful arms reached out, helping her cross the debris to firm ground.

The world was all wrong.

There were the two maples that stood in front of her house and yet now they stood alone, towering over nothing but debris. She thought she should cry but no tears came. The early morning air was chilly and dew sparkled across the meadow behind the farmhouse.

Correction, she thought numbly, the meadow that *used* to be behind the farmhouse. Now the meadow was just… There. The woods beyond, hills rising above, remained. It all seemed so strange. She saw birds flit in the trees along the creek. The light over the hills glowed pink and gold. It was a pretty sunrise….

People swarmed toward her. Neighbors, relieved faces, arms reaching for her, embracing her, asking a thousand questions that rolled past her.

"We were so worried—"

"We drove by and saw your house and called—"

"My family…" she kept asking.

Nobody'd talked to her family—phones were out all over the place, but they told her the town was okay, shaken, no deaths reported, no buildings down. She couldn't believe it. She had to see for herself. The need to get there, right now, right this minute, burned through her.

A paramedic broke through, descended on her. She made light of her cuts and scrapes. There was an angry-looking scratch on her arm that she hadn't even realized was there.

"I'm fine," she said for the fourth time.

Her eyes caught Jake's briefly from a distance. A paramedic was checking him over, too. He looked different in the new day. Still dangerously sexy, maybe more so, even with grime from the contact with debris covering his clothes. Her heart gave a peculiar wrench and she struggled to keep her perspective. Get a grip, she reminded herself.

Then her mind swerved. *The skull in the rose garden...*

The thought of what she'd found, just before Jake Malloy and everything else that seemed so unreal about yesterday had hit, tumbled over her. The box still in her hand seemed oddly hot.

"Keely!"

Oh, God, her mom.

Keely wheeled in time to see her mother all but flying across the dew-laden grass, her father beyond her still getting out of their car where they'd pulled over on the side of the road between emergency vehicles.

In seconds, her mother's arms were around her. Her parents were okay. Her sister was okay, she found out quickly, as were her brothers and their families. Everyone was okay.

"But are *you* okay?" her mother repeated. "Are you really okay? To be trapped there, under the house, all that time and we didn't know— We couldn't call and the road was closed. There was a rock fall blocking the highway, no one could get through last night and after they cleared it they weren't letting anyone but emergency vehicles come through till just a little while ago."

Her parents had been in their own hell worrying about her just as she had about them. Her mother held her face in her hands now, looking up to her because she was smaller than Keely. Roxie Bennett's petite body, still slim despite her sixty-two years, had always been the one Keely had wished she'd inherited instead of her father's taller bone structure. Howard Bennett stood behind her mother now, watching her with the identical anxious look as in her mother's eyes.

"I'm okay, I promise." She hugged both of them again. "I wasn't alone, though. I had help." She turned, searched the faces of people still milling around the devastated property. "But I need to talk to the police. I need to—"

She couldn't see Jake Malloy anywhere.

An emergency triage had been set up at the community center in town. They'd taken a look at the cuts on his back, cleaned them out and applied some salve. Jake was in and out in under an hour. There was a serious amount of media attention, reporters roaming all over the parking lot and throughout the small center.

He hadn't said goodbye to Keely and that bothered him even when he knew it was for the best. They'd helped each other through a bad night. He'd done what he could to keep her safe, and even if he hadn't kept her safe from him, he could remedy things now, do the right thing, stay away from her.

She was with her family now. She didn't need him. He'd taken the trip into town with the paramedics just to save any awkwardness. She'd have probably offered him a ride with her family. No sense dragging things out that way, though he realized now he'd left so quickly he hadn't stopped to retrieve any of his luggage out of his smashed car. He'd have to find a way back later, see if he could pry a door open and get into the trunk.

The image of her in that bright yellow T-shirt when she'd opened the door of her farmhouse to him the evening before wormed its way into his mind. He knew what was under that T-shirt and those worn jeans now and her perfect body was forever branded on his mind. How she looked, how she smelled, how she felt beneath his hands...

She'd trusted him. Despite everything, she'd trusted him.

Don't go there, don't go there, don't go there.

Ruthlessly, he cut off all thoughts of Keely Schiffer. He didn't have time for a relationship. Or the desire for one. He was hanging out in this one-horse town for a month, if he could stand it that long, and that was it. He didn't want to leave a broken heart behind, and no matter what Keely said about not planning to get married again, she wasn't the type to fool around without risking her heart. She was soft and sweet under that fragile shell of hers.

He was hard and bitter and she didn't need him in her life.

The community center was maybe a half mile from the house he'd rented across from the Food-way. He skirted a reporter with a cameraman interviewing a woman clutching a small boy in her arms. She was wearing jeans and a ripped shirt with no shoes.

"He was outside playing in the creek when the quake hit," he heard the woman saying. "I went out looking for him and I couldn't find him. I couldn't find him all night." She started crying. "We found him wandering up the road this morning. He told me he was in a cloud of light, a red cloud of light."

"A number of residents called in reporting fire in the hollows. Do you think he was near a fire?"

"I don't know," the mother said. "I'm just glad my baby's safe. I didn't see any fire."

The journalist turned to face the camera.

"Despite numerous reports of fires and reddish lights or haze across the county throughout the evening hours, so far emergency personnel have yet to locate any fires. In this tiny rural county of fifteen thousand that was the epicenter of the four-point-three quake, the news is good with damage consisting chiefly of fallen chimneys, broken windows and rattled dishes. Ninety-eight people have reported for treatment at the temporary triage here at the Haven Community Center and over a hundred more have been treated at the local hospital. No deaths have been—"

The heavy door of the community center slammed shut behind him, cutting off the reporter's final words. He headed for the rental house, about a quarter of a mile up the road.

He hadn't paid much attention to the town of Haven the day before driving in. He'd been in a hurry. Why, he had no idea. He had nothing to do but twiddle his damn thumbs here. He was in the middle of nowhere and the city seemed far, far away. Haven was surrounded by thick woods full of oak and hickory and walnut, broken by the sloped pastures and quaint farmhouses of the Appalachian mountains. The town itself wasn't much more than a restored town square with a beautiful courthouse. Antique-style lampposts stood like sentinels along the cobbled sidewalks lined with businesses—a dress shop, a clock repair shop, lawyer offices, a craft and consignment retailer and a diner called Almost Heaven. A few side streets held a mix of Victorian-era homes. Another set of side streets held more modern brick businesses. A sign indicated a school up another road.

The reporter seemed correct in his statements about the damage in Haven. Main Street on the square led him back out to the quiet two-lane highway. After the demolishment of Keely's farmhouse he'd witnessed firsthand, he'd expected more devastation in town, but he saw little evidence of it.

What he saw as he reached the steps of the rental house was Keely, her slender, sexy, stop-traffic body unfolding from the passenger seat of a small sedan in front of the little grocery store across the narrow highway. He jammed his fingers into his front pocket, pulled out the house key he'd gotten from Keely what seemed like an eternity ago before all hell broke loose at the farmhouse.

He strode up the scuffed wooden steps of the house and onto the narrow front porch, refusing to look Keely's way. He had his own problems; she had hers. They'd had one night together, born of desperation and survival, and it was over.

And just because he could still taste her, feel her, smell her in his memory, didn't mean he'd get to ever do it again in reality.

Move on. Detach and focus.

It was three hours later when he managed to track down a car rental place within walking distance. He was able to rent a car there and he drove back to Keely's farm. The Jag was right where he'd left it—smashed under a tree. He'd saved and saved to buy the damn thing. Now it was toast.

The passenger side door was usable, so he pulled his bag of toiletries from the back then got the trunk open to get his suitcase and laptop. He stashed his things in the rental car.

The farm was quiet, deserted now after all the activity that morning. Even the equipment the rescuers had used had been moved off, no doubt needed elsewhere, as were the emergency workers. Despite what good shape the town appeared to be in, contrasting with the utter destruction of Keely's home, he'd been told by the car rental clerk that a number of roads were closed due to fallen rocks and trees.

There was a wooden sign swinging from a chain on a post near the road. Sugar Run Farm, Est. 1882.

Keely wasn't going to get over the loss of her house as quick as he'd gotten over his car, not considering the family history here. An old well house, looking like something out of a photograph, stood to one side of the ruined farmhouse, covered with ivy. The ground to one side was plowed, ready for a big vegetable garden. An empty chicken coop proclaimed this had been a real working farm in days gone by.

It was almost impossible for him to imagine the family history in this place. His father had taken off when he was nine, and after that, his mother had scraped by the best she could. He'd started working when he was fourteen. By the time he could really help her, she'd died of cancer. Extended family on either side was virtually nonexistent. Despite the rural nature of the state, he'd spent little time outside the city limits unless it was to go white-water rafting on one of West Virginia's wild rivers. He'd always headed straight back for the city afterward. He was comfortable there, with the traffic, the noise, the people who surrounded him but left him alone.

He'd just about always gone solo, so things weren't much different now. Keely was living in a whole different world. He didn't belong in it, but he felt an odd, edgy tightness as he thought of her with her family after they'd been rescued. The country was quiet, and his mind didn't know what to do with it. If he was supposed to find peace here, it wasn't working so far.

Restless, he walked toward the house, circling the pile of rubble. There was a barn beyond the house, and a meadow bottom leading down to a creek with woods beyond. Picturesque, despite the devastation, with spring wildflowers waving in the light air. Cows dotted a hillside in another distant direction. The breeze kicked up and carried the sound of a moo.

There was fresh-turned dirt in a small garden that lay just to the rear of the house, too, the soil still moist despite the bright sunshine. There was, in fact, a hole…a deep one.

Something trickled down his spine, an awareness of… Being watched.

He turned slowly, saw nothing but road and woods and hills beyond, heard nothing but the sigh of wind on the Appalachian air. His instincts told him otherwise, though. Somebody was here. He reached for his gun, held it down at his side. He'd replaced the bullets back at the rental house, on R&R but still operating on automatic.

Somebody was here and something was going on, he just didn't know what. He'd lay odds someone had been digging out behind Keely's house this afternoon…. Why?

He heard a noise and knew it came from the barn. He was maybe fifteen feet from it. No cell phone, no backup. No authority, frankly. An engine roared.

A thundering crash shocked him and he barely threw himself out of the way as a truck rammed straight through the barn doors, screaming toward the road. Jake hit the ground hard, rolled, scrambled to his feet in time to see nothing but the white tailgate of a late-model pickup disappearing around the sharp bend.

Chapter 7

"Did you hear about Jud Peterson?"

"No. Could you grab the other end of this shelf?"
Keely focused on the task at hand, only half listening to her friend and part-time assistant, who was usually in the office, but today she needed all available hands on restocking duty. The store was a wreck inside with things toppled off shelves in every aisle, but it was open. She had an obligation, being the only full-service grocer in town, but beyond that it was keeping her mind off what had happened to the farmhouse. And what had happened with Jake Malloy.

Lise Tanner was not deterred even as she helped Keely get a lower shelf back on its tracks. "I heard he called a paranormal detective."

Now that got Keely's attention. "What?"

"He said he got surrounded by some kind of weird red light out on Boscastle Road last night. Said it came down on the ground right over top of him and he ran and it followed him everywhere he went, like he was running in a ball of red light."

"He was drunk. He's always drunk." Jud got picked up about every other weekend for public intoxication. Everybody knew that. He was nice enough in between times and scraped out a living doing odd jobs around town. Keely hired him occasionally herself out of charity—he'd gone to school with Ray.

"Probably." Lise propped a box of detergent back up on a lower shelf. "He's an ass." Lise had dated Jud one summer in high school. Back then, he'd been a cute bad boy and Lise had sown her wild oats for a few months. "But you know he's not the only one saying weird stuff happened last night when the quake struck. Like, UFOs or something."

Keely felt a rush of something cold go down her spine. She'd seen a weird reddish light, too, and there'd been that strange way Ray's box had tumbled nearly into her hand right before they'd gotten rescued.

But unidentified flying objects or something paranormal…

That was just nonsense. Had to be. She'd been in shock, scared, and probably something electrical had snapped at the farmhouse when the quake struck, which would explain the flash of light, just like Jake had said.

And as for the box, the only thing weird about it was that Ray had bothered to plan that far in advance to give her a birthday gift. But then, didn't everyone do something out of character sometimes? Like, herself, for example. Last night.

Don't go there, she reminded herself even as her pulse jumped all by its rebellious self. A tingly feeling way down low reminded her that she'd had a good time, too.

Now she had to pay the price. Regret.

"Ray left me a present," she said abruptly.

The front door of the store dinged as another customer came in.

"What do you mean, a present?" Lise finished putting up the last box of detergent and stood, brushing off her jeans.

How she managed to look perfect no matter

what she was doing was a mystery. Keely'd showered and changed into fresh clothes at her mom's before coming over to the store—against her mother's objections that she should rest after her "ordeal"—and yet she was already a mess from crawling around on the floor picking up grocery items.

Lise, on the other hand, looked like a fashion plate, per usual. She was three years older than Keely and her family had gone to church with hers, so Keely had often gotten her hand-me-downs. She'd never looked as good in them as Lise had.

Especially today when she was tired and felt hungover from stress and grief over the farmhouse. Everyone she loved was alive, though. That was what mattered.

Keely pushed up from her knees.

"A birthday present. Can you believe it? He bought me something, wrapped it up, left the box in the cookie jar. I found it yesterday."

Lise's perfectly manicured brows lifted. "Really? That's interesting. Hmm."

"Yeah. Hmm." Keely tried real hard not to say anything negative but gave up. "Maybe he thought I was going to find out he'd been sleeping around with Alexa Donner."

"Or Judy Applegate or Cherry Whitehead or—"

"Okay, okay." Keely held her hand up.

"I don't know why you get uptight whenever you start to say anything bad about him. He was a jerk, and personally I'm not sorry he's dead."

"Oh, my God, balance your chakra." Keely waved her hand in a zigzag motion. Mary O'Hurley used to be her best friend in kindergarten, but now she read palms and tarot cards out of her house and at the occasional school carnival. Even if Keely didn't believe in any of that stuff—truth was, Mary didn't, either—she'd picked up some of the New Age jargon just for fun.

"Ray needed something balanced and it wasn't his chakra," Lise said. "Maybe he even killed somebody! What are you going to say then?"

Keely'd tried to make a police report about the skull she'd found in the rose bed but every available state trooper was otherwise occupied on emergency detail. They told her they'd call her back later today and get out to the scene as soon as they had the manpower.

A skull in her garden wasn't top priority under the extraordinary circumstances.

"We don't know that," she pointed out. Not that she could think of any other explanation. She'd even thought about getting out the phone book and checking up on all the women, at least the ones she knew about, who Ray'd slept with.

But that was a little too embarrassing. *Um, hello, this is Ray's widow, and I found a skull in my garden. Just wondering if you're okay....*

Right.

Besides, she'd have heard if any of the women he'd slept with had gone missing. They were mostly local girls. The only one she knew about from Charleston was Cherry Whitehead, and surely she'd have heard about her if she was missing, too. Their local network news came out of the city.

Lise rolled her eyes. She was always quick to condemn Ray, which was one of the reasons Keely hated to say anything bad about him. Lise said enough.

Or maybe it just reminded her of how stupid she'd been to marry him. She had judgment trouble when it came to men. If anyone's energy centers were out of whack and needed balancing, it was hers.

"Whatever." Lise waved off the topic of Ray, to Keely's relief. "Now, about your birthday—"

"I don't want to do anything."

"Your mom said she was going to fix dinner at her house for everybody. Come on. That means I don't have to cook." Lise's husband, Tom, worked for the town and seemed pretty decent as far as men went. They'd been high-school sweethearts. Aside from that minor episode with Jud, Lise had better judgment in men than Keely. "Besides, you're staying there now anyway, aren't you?"

"Do you hate me? No." The thought of living with her parents made Keely want to choke. She loved them, but live with them? No, double no, triple no. They would drive her crazy, fussing over her. They were also seriously committed to getting her remarried and eventually they'd get back to their mission when the shock of the quake passed. "I'm going to use the apartment over the store. I haven't been able to rent it out, and now that's a good thing. But yes, okay, I'll go back over there for dinner." She wouldn't want to disappoint her mom about that, at least, though she knew it would mean a huge gathering of family and friends, and she wasn't really feeling up to it.

"So did you open the present?"

Back to that topic.

Keely shook her head. "Maybe later. I don't know. I still have it." She'd stuck it in her office desk drawer when she'd come over to the store earlier from her parents' house. Lise had brought clothes and a few necessities—Keely could get anything else she needed straight from the store shelves. She felt funny about opening the box. It was on the wrong side of strange, getting a gift from the grave. "I have a lot of other stuff on my mind."

"I'm sorry about the farmhouse." Lise touched her arm. "You were always so attached to it, and I know how much you wanted it. You can rebuild, you know. Insurance money. A new house will be so much easier to live in."

"I liked the old house."

"I know. I'm just glad you're okay, that's all." Lise pulled her into a quick hug then leaned back. "Everything's going to be okay, you know."

"I know," she lied.

"You're alive, that's all that matters. I'm glad you weren't alone. You haven't said much about this Jake Malloy guy who was with you."

And she wasn't going to. She'd given Lise the *Reader's Digest* version of her night trapped in the cellar, the same story she'd given her parents. Sometimes she told her friends everything and sometimes she didn't. This time it was the latter. She sensed that Lise didn't always tell her everything, either.

"There's nothing to tell. Look, it's nearly three o'clock. Weren't you supposed to get your mom at three? She wants to go help out at the community center, right? And you were supposed to give her a ride."

"Oh, yeah. Thanks. I wasn't watching the time." Lise narrowed her eyes. "But don't think I didn't catch that. I want to hear about this guy and you can't put me off forever."

"He's old and fat and has a wart," Keely said with a straight face. Lise could be as bad as her parents about trying to set her up. She was sure all Keely needed was a good man, like Tom. "He was nice, that's all. I was glad I wasn't alone all night. End of story."

"Hey, boss lady." Tammy Draper, the clerk, called her from the front of the store. "Somebody's looking for you."

Keely followed her friend up to the front of the store.

Tammy was ringing up another customer. There'd been a run on bottled water and Keely noticed it was again the most popular item at the cash register. A lot of the people out in the country had wells that ran on electricity and power was out in half the county. She counted herself lucky they still had it at the store and that the phones were working.

Bright afternoon light spilled in from outside

and at first all she could see was a lean shadow against the glaring sun on the glass windows of the storefront. Then he turned and her eyes adjusted and the rest of her body went haywire, including her brain.

"I didn't mean for them to call you up here," Jake Malloy said. "I just wanted to know if you were in the store. I would have come to find you. I'd like to speak with you privately, if possible."

Privately? He wanted to speak to her privately?

Keely swallowed hard. Dammit. He was just as melt-your-knees hot as she'd remembered, and she'd rather not have even remembered much less had to face him. Unlike Lise, she looked like crap. Not that she cared what Jake Malloy thought of her.

Okay, she cared.

Her brain was definitely out of control. She had to fight a flashback of his hands all over her body. She'd lost her cool with him completely last night. Not again.

Deliberately, her gaze locked on him and held. She could handle this. He looked amazing in another plain T-shirt and jeans, but so what? Her insides quivered and she told herself she was probably just hungry. She hadn't stopped for lunch.

Then she remembered her friend, standing next to her. This was going to be trouble.

"Hi. I'm Lise Tanner, Keely's friend." Lise stuck out her manicured hand. "And you are…"

"Jake Malloy." He took her hand, shook it.

"Ah." Lise gave Keely a long look, then turned an amused gaze back on Jake. "I heard about you. I didn't recognize you without your wart."

Jake's brow furrowed. "My what?"

Lise grinned. "I'll let Keely explain." She gave an airy wave. "I've got to go grab my mom. You, babe, have got some 'splaining to do with me, too. See you at dinner." She turned, then swiveled back. "Hey. I know you're new in town and everything. And we're all so grateful about how you were there for Keely last night. It's her birthday and we're having a big dinner over at her folks' tonight. Family, and a bunch of her friends and—"

Oh, no. Keely knew where this was going and she didn't like it.

"Lise—"

"You're a friend now, that's for sure. Please join us. Dinner's at seven. Home cooking. Keely's mom's the best. I know she'd want you to come. We all would."

If she could have crawled into a hole, Keely would have so been there.

"Keely can get you directions." Lise sported a smug grin. "If you don't get your pickup back from Dickie by tonight, call me and I'll send Tom after you."

She took off into the bright sun, the bell over the door dinging behind her. The store suddenly felt really small, like airplane-bathroom small, just Keely and the man she'd had, what felt like fantasy sex with last night.

And people were watching. She could feel Tammy's eyes boring into her back. Curious.

"I have an office in the rear," Keely said. She couldn't imagine what Jake Malloy wanted to speak to her about, but best to get it over with quickly before her imagination went nuts with possibilities. And no way was she discussing Lise's wart remark.

As for the dinner invitation…

"I'm sorry about my friend. Don't feel like you have to be polite about that. I'm sure you'd be bored stiff at my parents'."

Her office was the size of a beanbag, but at least when she stuck her foot in her mouth, which she was bound to do at any moment, it wouldn't be reported on the gossip tree. Her desk was noticeably cluttered with snacks propped on top of every stack of paperwork. Half-eaten packages of do- nuts, chocolate pretzels, gummy bears, candy bars, you name it. It was a constant temptation, working all day in a grocery store full of goodies.

Keely sank into the chair behind the desk and motioned Jake into the metal folding chair against the wall by the door. He shut the door first.

She hadn't really wanted the door shut.

He filled up the tiny space, his expression dark and intense.

"That was nice of your friend," he said finally. "But you don't have to worry. I wouldn't want to intrude on your birthday dinner."

She felt like a heel now, a total heel.

"It's not that." Awkward, awkward, awkward. "I didn't mean that you would be intruding. It's just… I thought we decided it'd be better if we just went our separate ways." The conversation had been bad enough this morning. She didn't want to have it again. "What was it you wanted to speak with me about?" she prompted. Hurry. Her foot was already halfway down her throat.

He watched her like he could see right into her head and knew she was full of crap.

"Are you doing all right?" he asked.

"I'm fine. And that's really kind of you to ask, but—" But she had lots of things to do in the store and if he didn't stop staring at her, she was going to hyperventilate. She resisted the urge to reach for a donut. Sugar was not the answer to her problem.

A lobotomy might be.

"I'm glad," he said.

"Are you okay?" Polite. She could be polite. That's all he was being. It wasn't like he could possibly really care how she was doing beyond the social nicety of it. He certainly hadn't stuck around for chitchat after they'd been rescued. "Everything all right with the house? It wasn't damaged in the quake, was it?" The thought abruptly occurred to her. If the house was messed up, the only other rental she had to offer was the apartment over the store and she didn't really want to give that up.

"The house is fine. I noticed a few things out of place, some things that must have fallen out of shelves. No big deal."

"Oh, good." Relief washed her. "So…"

She waited, let her gaze drift away nonchalantly though the truth was she couldn't handle holding his eyes directly, wondering how he could carry on this casual conversation with her as if they hadn't stripped their clothes off last night and had wildly explosive sex. Or was she the only one who'd felt that way about it?

That was not a good thought. She noticed how his lean muscled shoulders pushed the limits of his T-shirt. She remembered how powerful those shoulders had felt under her touch. That was not a good thought, either.

Her mouth watered and this time she really did pick up a donut.

"Want one?" she offered. "I skipped lunch. I'm hungry."

He shook his head. "I went out to your place this afternoon. I rented a car."

His smashed car. She'd almost forgotten about it.

She swallowed a bite of donut. "Great. I'm still sorry about your car."

"Not your fault."

The office phone rang. Keely gladly reached for it. "Well, if that's all, it's really busy here." To show how terribly busy she was, she said, "Foodway, Keely Schiffer here," quite officiously into the phone, put her barely eaten donut down, wiped her fingers on a paper towel she deftly ripped off a roll on the filing cabinet behind her, and grabbed a pen and pad of paper as if ready to take down very important information. She was busy. Multitasking. Official.

"Hey, girl, how you doing?" Mary's perky voice bubbled across the phone line.

"Fine. But shouldn't you already know that?" Keely couldn't resist teasing her friend. She'd only once let Mary read her palm and that time had scared her so badly, she'd never let her do it again. Mary'd told her there was a black cloud surrounding her aura and that she saw a man and a woman as shadowy figures who were going to hurt her. It'd been a few years ago and it was right after that when Keely had discovered Ray was cheating on her.

She'd reminded Mary she'd only seen a man and one woman when it should have been at least four or five women.

"Brat," Mary said. "I'm just glad you're okay. I was having the weirdest feeling about you and I had to be sure."

"No more aura stuff," Keely interrupted. She avoided Jake's gaze though she could feel him watching her. He hadn't left the office.

He was waiting—for what?

"It's probably just your mom freaking me out when she told me about your house and everything," Mary said. "She told me you were at the store and I know I'll see you tonight, but I'm worried about you. I just had to hear your voice. I keep feeling like something's wrong with you."

"Nothing's wrong."

"You know, I saw those red lights last night that everybody's talking about," Mary said. "Did you? And today, Patsy Renniker came over and asked me to do a tarot reading on her. You know she has me do one once a week and I swear even an earthquake isn't going to stop her, and I got so scared, I told her to go home. She's got cancer. I know she's got cancer. I mean, I don't know that but it's like I could see it when I started doing her cards. I told her to go to the doctor, right away."

"You can't know that."

"It freaked me out, Keely. You know I don't ever tell anybody anything bad when I do a reading. I never thought anything bad before. I just tell everybody they're going to live to be a hundred. Good stuff. But now— It's like it's for real now. I'm not making it up anymore. And I keep getting this feeling about you."

"I'm fine." Actually, Mary was starting to freak her out. "What about you? What about your place?"

"Nothing messed up but my new gazebo. Fell over, completely, probably because *somebody* hadn't finished nailing the sides right. Eighty-five percent finished and he lets it sit there for the past six months. Now it's ruined."

"Eighty-five percent syndrome," Keely said. "Men only build things to eighty-five percent completion."

"No kidding. I get eighty-five percent on the way to an orgasm and Danny's finished," Mary said.

Keely started to laugh then accidentally caught Jake's drop-dead hot eyes when she leaned her head back and she swallowed so hard she nearly choked. No eighty-five percent completion rate for Jake.

He'd made her way too happy way too many times last night. Effortlessly, it seemed.

And still he sat here in her office, all steady and dangerously sexy-looking, as if he was waiting for something. He wasn't finished, whatever it was he'd come to speak to her about. And as long as he was here, she was going to have sex on the brain and Mary wasn't helping.

"I have to go. I'll call you later, okay?" She put the phone down after Mary'd said goodbye. "Um, is there something else you want with me?"

"I think something's going on, and I think you need to know."

"Didn't we already discuss this?" She felt a trickle of sweat between her breasts and the air-conditioning was working, so that wasn't it. "It was just a one-night stand. I'm sure you've had them before. Who hasn't?" Liar.

"I wasn't talking about last night. Or about us."

Heat flushed her entire body. "Oh." Could she possibly be more stupid and one-track-minded?

She had a serious case of falling in lust with him, that's all. He was drop-dead, steal-your-breath handsome. But so what. Ray had been a looker, too. She mustered her self-control. Again. She forced herself to look for flaws, and found a few. His nose was slightly crooked. There was a scar along his jaw, and another one near his temple. He lived hard. He was a cop.

And there was, suddenly, a deadly serious cop look in his eyes.

A nervous prickle moved up her spine. "So what were you talking about?"

"Is there some reason," he said quietly, "that someone would be digging around in the back of your farmhouse?"

Chapter 8

Keely went from a very pretty blush to white in the time it took Jake to blink. The bad feeling that had come calling out at her farm settled into permanent residence in his gut.

"What's wrong?"

"Nothing." She got up out of her chair, paced in the very tiny space behind her desk as if suddenly ready to crawl out of her skin. She stopped, her strangely desperate eyes locked on his. "Did you see anyone?"

"They tried to run me down, or at least they

would have if I hadn't gotten out of the way. They were in a pickup truck in your barn."

"What?"

"The barn doors were shut and they just came smashing through the doors like a bat out of hell."

"Oh, my God."

"Know anybody with a white pickup?"

"I have a white pickup!"

"Where is it?"

"It's still at Dickie's. The mechanic," she explained.

"Are you sure?"

"I can find out. But wait. What's this about the ground being dug up?"

"There was freshly turned dirt in back of the house, where some pots of rosebushes were sitting like you were going to plant them. It was still damp and there was a hole. This isn't something that happened when the rescue guys were out there." And whoever had been digging, they hadn't wanted him to find them still on the place.

But why?

She turned even whiter, if that was possible. "Any police crime-scene tape, anything like that?"

Crime-scene tape?

"No. Why?"

She shook her head. "I was just wondering."

Just *wondering* if there was crime-scene tape around her house? Nope, he wasn't buying that blow-off.

"That wasn't the police barreling out of your barn, Keely."

She frowned. "Yes, I know." She looked confused, like she was struggling to put it all together. "I just was wondering if that was something separate from what you saw dug up. But that doesn't make sense, does it?"

None of it made sense to him.

He didn't want to be worried about her, but he was, and it was at least a welcome replacement to the unallowable beat of desire that had pulsed inside him when she'd jumped to the wrong conclusion about what he wanted to discuss.

She was wearing a weathered West Virginia University blue-and-gold T-shirt and a clean pair of jeans, and she looked more like she was about twenty-one than… Maybe thirty? Today was her birthday, he remembered.

She sat back down and picked up the phone, jabbed numbers in. "Hi, this is—" Her head turned up at Jake. "Do you mind?"

"Yes."

Exasperation tightened her features when he didn't leave, which she obviously wanted him to do. He wasn't leaving till he knew what was going on, why she'd reacted the way she had to what he'd told her, and if she was in any kind of danger.

He shouldn't give a damn. He'd slept with her, but so what? It was a one-night stand, just like she'd so pointedly said. Clearly, he was insane, but he wasn't leaving till he was sure she was all right. She was scared, and like last night, he was going to be there for her till he was sure she was safe.

As soon as he was sure of that, he could go back across the road and forget about her completely.

"—Keely Schiffer," she was saying into the phone. She'd swiveled her chair around as if by simply ignoring him, he'd disappear. "I called earlier about making a report. I was wondering— No, I know you said they were too busy to get out here to take my statement yet. But I was wondering if troopers had gone out to the farm? Jake Malloy told me that there had been some digging out there today. And someone tried to run him down coming out of my barn. Smashed the barn doors coming out."

A statement? She'd called earlier about making a statement to the cops. Jake watched her, the bad feeling gnawing harder at him. He remembered the way she'd seemed almost…desperate for him to come in her house the day before, how she'd seemed to not want to be alone. It had been a passing impression at the time, but now he wondered if it was connected to this statement she was waiting to make to the police. Something had happened at the farmhouse before he'd arrived, before the quake.

Something that had scared her.

Again, bad sign that he wasn't walking out the door. He would need to make his own statement to the police, though.

But the longer he hung around, the more he could be sucked in to whatever was going on in Keely's life. What if he did just walk away and then something happened to her? He couldn't live with that. He'd just have to be careful, watch his back while he was watching hers, and not get sucked in.

Keely's shoulders remained tight, tense. "Evidence could be disturbed," she was saying. "What if— What if it goes missing? I mean—" She pressed her hand into her forehead. "Okay. I know. You'll get out there as soon as you can. I know that." Another beat. "Jake Malloy." She gave the address of the rental house. "I'm sure he'd be happy to make a statement, as well. Thank you." She put the phone down.

"The cops been out there?"

"Not yet. She said someone was supposed to be out there this afternoon. They'll want a statement from you, too."

"Want to tell me what's going on?"

"No."

"You look scared, Keely."

"I'm okay." She didn't look okay, or sound okay, but she was damn sure going to try and fake it. She stood, walked around the desk and reached for the doorknob. She was throwing him out of her office.

He rose, fast, and put his hand over hers, stilling hers before she could turn the knob. She lifted bright, still scared but faking-it-for-all-she-was-worth eyes to his. He couldn't shake the bad feeling about what was happening to her.

"Look, thank you for telling me," she said. "Thank you for your concern. But this is my business. It's police business."

"The police don't seem to be helping."

"They're busy, that's all. We had an earthquake, remember?"

Oh, he remembered. And he couldn't help catching the defensive thread in her voice, or the way it slightly shook.

"Yes, I remember."

The flash of awkward intimacy in her eyes was his immediate and torturous reward. The apples of her cheeks pinkened again. He remembered how sweet-soft her skin had been….

He veered the subject away from that thought. "I'm a cop, too, Keely."

"You're not a cop here. And I have a store that needs my attention." Her voice came out slightly breathy.

She was upset about whatever was going on back at her farm, but she wasn't unaffected by his nearness, too. The buzz of awareness that had started humming between them last night hadn't diminished any—but she wasn't that same naive-seeming, friendly woman. She'd opened up to him last night in ways he'd never expected, and now she was all closed up again in whatever shell it was that she used to armor herself against the world. Or maybe just men.

And maybe this thing between them had a mind of its own because he could tell she was fighting it just like he was. And not doing so good. Like him on that, too.

"I just don't like it that you're scared," he admitted quietly. "I want to help if I can." Something about her was softening him, even if he didn't like it. He brought his hand up over her arm, barely realizing he was doing it.

"I'd thank you for that, but I'm not scared so much as I'm mad." Her voice rose.

"What are you mad about, Keely?"

He had a feeling she was holding a lot inside. She was sweet and good and didn't want to speak ill of the dead, but she'd been hurt in her life and she had to have some anger inside over it. He knew all about holding anger inside. Maybe he didn't want her to end up like him, bitter and isolated.

"I want to be your friend," he said. Friendship. That was easy. He could do friendship. "Tell me why you're mad. You deserve to be mad, about lots of things. You lost your house. You lost your husband. Maybe you've lost other things I don't even know about."

She blinked and he could see something moist in her eyes. "Yeah. I'm mad about my house falling down around me. You know how old that house was?"

"How old?"

"A hundred years. A hundred years old! And now it's gone. I'm the fourth generation in my family to live in that house, and the last one now."

"There were a lot of things in that house. Pictures, antiques. Probably a lot of sentimental value in those things, memories."

A tear swelled in her gaze. She nodded. "My great-grandmother's butter churns. My grandmother's nativity collection. My great-grandfather's Civil War rifle. The high chair my grandfather made for my father, carved it himself. It's all gone. And it just seems so senseless." Her shoulders sagged slightly. "A lot of things in life are senseless."

"I had a friend die recently," Jake said. "He was young, smart, had his whole life ahead of him." He sighed. "It wasn't just senseless, it was unnecessary."

"How'd he die?"

"We were undercover, cracking a drug ring. Things went bad. Brian got shot. The damn house was on fire, meth everywhere. There was a kid in the house and there was no way I could take out both of them at once. I saved the kid. Before I could go back in, the house blew." His chest banded. Guilt threatened to swallow him. They'd called him a hero for saving that little girl. He hadn't felt like much of a hero.

"I'm sorry." Her voice lowered, softened. "I'm so sorry."

He could have drowned in her eyes. Sympathy.

He didn't want it, but the understanding in her gaze, understanding of pain and loss, felt good in some unexpected way at the same time that it made him uncomfortable.

"You lost your husband," he pointed out, changing the topic.

She said nothing.

"Talk to me, Keely. Tell me what happened to him."

"He made a bad decision, drove off in a downpour, flood conditions. His car got washed away at a low-water bridge. He drowned."

Now he knew why she'd been so adamant yesterday about the dangerous driving conditions in the storm.

"I'm mad about that," she said suddenly, sharply. "He knew better. He had bad judgment, about a lot of things."

"Did he hurt you, Keely?" He cared, more than he liked.

"He didn't hit me or anything, if that's what you mean."

"A man doesn't have to hit a woman to hurt her."

She was silent for a long breath. "He didn't work at all for years, went to school, but never finished. Then he hurt his back on the farm and

decided he was going to be a writer. Supposedly.
He never sold anything, or even tried to get anything published that I know about. He put us in
debt when he bought the store. Then he didn't
work it like he said he would. He was always gone.
He'd come back with inventory for the store,
antiques, small things for the jewelry case by the
register, but I never knew where he got them. I was
always scared they were stolen because I couldn't
see where he had the money to buy anything. He
said he got stuff at estate auctions, but I didn't
believe him. And he cheated on me." Her chin
lifted. "More than once. And I didn't do anything
about it. I didn't leave him. I'm mad about that,
too. I'm mad at myself."

"He's gone now. You get to start over." It blew his
mind to think someone would cheat on this beautiful woman. No wonder she didn't like promises.
She'd had plenty of them broken…important ones.

"Maybe. I'm mad that there's something buried
in my garden back at the farm."

She bit her lip and he knew she hadn't meant to
tell him that much. His mind stumbled over what
she'd said, locked on.

No wonder she'd been nervous the day before.

"What do you think was buried there?"

He kept his hand on her arm. She stared back at him for a long beat then looked aside.

"I found a skull, a human skull, yesterday when I was getting ready to plant some roses." Her voice was low, slightly trembly now. "Ray's the one who dug that garden up last fall, tore some old bushes out. Maybe he put that skull there. Maybe my husband was a murderer. And maybe it's gone now because the state troopers didn't get out there soon enough. I'm mad about that, too." She gave a little laugh that didn't sound like she thought anything was funny. "I shouldn't get started on all I'm mad about."

"Maybe you should get it out more often." He waited until she looked back at him. "Stop keeping the anger inside." He was one to talk, he realized. "You don't have anything to be ashamed of, you know. You didn't do anything wrong. It was your husband who did."

If her husband wasn't already on his way to hell, he'd have been happy to give him a send-off. If it wasn't bad enough what Ray had done when he was alive, maybe he'd also left her a terrible secret to deal with after his death. A surge of protectiveness toward her rose inside him.

"I was a coward. I didn't want to admit I'd made a mistake, so I stayed with him."

Ah, hell. He wanted to pull her into his arms. He wanted to comfort her, make her feel better somehow.

"You're awfully hard on yourself."

"Somebody's got to be."

"Then maybe you should take a break, give somebody else a turn. And if nobody else steps up to the plate, maybe you don't deserve it." He'd seen her parents with her. Her friends. He didn't think anyone else was going to be hard on Keely the way she was on herself. People cared about her. She just didn't care about herself so much.

"You barely know me."

He realized he was still stroking his fingers up and down her arm and that she'd let go of the doorknob. She wasn't trying to escape him. He didn't mean to, but he pulled her closer and she let him.

Her nose and lips and seductive apple scent were that close, a breath away. He could kiss her and she wouldn't stop him, he sensed.

I want to be your friend. That was what he'd told her.

"I think we level-jumped on our relationship a little last night," he said. He forcibly made himself let go of her arm, take a half step back in the cramped space of her office. Strangers to lovers in a matter of hours. It was clouding the issue at hand, which was making sure Keely was safe. "I get to be concerned about you now, and I *am* concerned. Someone was out there at your farm today. Someone was looking for something. Who knew about you finding it?"

She straightened her shoulders, seemed to be shoring up her defenses, too, as if she was just as aware that things had almost gotten out of hand again.

"The police. My family and friends." She shrugged. "That's all. It's not something I really want to spread around."

"Your family and friends might have told someone. Other people might have overheard. Did you tell your parents back at the farm this morning?" They'd been surrounded by rescue workers then. Anyone could have overheard.

"No, at least not the whole story. I didn't tell them till later, back at their house when I called the police. But they could have mentioned it to someone, I guess. I want to go out to the farm. I want to see if the skull is still there."

"That wouldn't be safe, Keely."

"I guess. But I want to see what I can salvage from the house, too."

"Not safe," he repeated firmly. "No guessing

about it. Someone was out there. And the dirt was freshly turned. See what you can salvage after the police are finished—they won't want you touching anything till then anyway. Someone's interested in what you found. Someone besides the police. And you know who that would be."

Someone who knew about the murder wanted it covered up.

"You're right. I know that. I won't go out there."

She looked scared enough that he believed her, but that didn't mean she was safe.

"But then…" She frowned. Her eyes lit slightly. "If there's somebody looking for it, then that would mean it wasn't Ray."

She didn't want to believe her husband had been a murderer. He could understand that. She was ashamed of Ray's actions, even though she wasn't responsible for them.

"Or it means Ray didn't act alone," he pointed out. That seemed more likely.

She swallowed hard and her mouth set grimly. "Yeah, that's a possibility, too."

"You should be careful," he said.

"I don't know anything. Whatever happened, whether it was Ray or someone else who put that skull there, I don't know anything about it. I just know Ray dug that garden up last fall. The ground out there wasn't touched till yesterday when I got ready to plant the roses. I don't know why he wanted to pull the bushes out last fall. He knew I wasn't going to plant anything new till spring, but he insisted and said he'd plant the roses for me, too. It wasn't really like him to do something in advance like that, before it had to be done, or to work in the garden at all. He had a bad back."

He'd bought her a birthday present in advance, too. Jake wondered if she'd opened that little box. But a gift from her dead husband seemed private. He hesitated to ask about it, but what if it was somehow connected to the murder?

"Maybe you know something and don't realize it, or maybe someone might just think you know something. You should be careful. Have you opened that present he left for you?"

She froze. "No."

"What if it has something to do with the murder?"

She gasped. "I don't think so. He wouldn't leave me a present that had anything to do with a murder."

"He left you a skull."

"We don't know that!"

Not yet. But Jake wasn't taking anything for granted.

"I'll open it later," she said quietly. "I'll give it to the police if it looks suspicious."

He nodded. "Thank you." He didn't like the anxious light in her eyes. "Where are you staying?"

"There's an apartment over the store. I'll be living there for now. The building is secure," she added. "The apartment can only be reached through the store, and the store has locks and I can lock the apartment, too."

Someone didn't have to get inside to get to her. They could catch her outside at night, or worse, set the building on fire. Anything was possible.

"Good. Don't forget." He reached for the door now. He was in too deep already and if he didn't get out of here, he might get in deeper. He might touch her again, and he might not be able to resist kissing her if he did.

"Umm...Jake?"

He looked back. She looked incredible, her spun-gold hair messy, bundled up on top of her head and falling down in rebellious tendrils that caressed her cheeks. She looked tired, too. Stressed out.

"Thank you."

"For what?"

"For being my friend." She chewed her lower

lip and conflicted shadow passed over her gaze. She sighed, lowered her lashes to avoid his eyes while she continued on, blurting the next words. "I lied. I've never had a one-night stand before."

His hand slipped out, tipped her chin, while he valiantly resisted the urge to pull her to him and kiss her.

"I already knew that," he said.

He saw the way she fought for control. Her eyes brimmed, emotion threatening to spill out, but she blinked it back. "Okay. I just wanted to say thank you for being my friend because, well, because it's not like I share that kind of thing with just anyone. I'd really like it if we could be friends."

Right. Friends. No problem. It had been his own idea.

"Of course," he lied, to himself, to her. But he'd make it true. "I promise. We're friends."

She stared at him. "I don't like promises."

"I don't break mine."

A long, achy silence weighted the room.

"I almost believe you." She stepped back now. He dropped his hand. "If you want to, it'd be nice if you came to dinner tonight. My parents wanted to meet you, and Lise is right, you're new in town. Haven is a friendly place. You haven't had a very good welcome to it. And you *are* one of my friends now."

He should have said no. What good could come of getting more involved in Keely's life? If he hadn't come to Haven, if he hadn't rented a house from her, if he hadn't had to go out to her farm to get the key, if his car hadn't been crushed by that tree, if he hadn't happened to be there in her house when the quake had struck—

If he'd believed in things like fate, it'd be easy to think he was in Keely's life for a reason, and that that reason was bigger than whatever fears he had that were making him want to say no. He didn't believe in fate. But his insides twisted with a sense of urgency, and all reasoning vanished when she was near.

"It won't be a huge crowd or anything," she added. "Just my family and a few friends. But no present, okay? I know it's my birthday, but I don't want you to get me a present."

His well-famed self-discipline that had gotten him out alive from numerous dangerous situations was failing him badly. And he didn't mean the danger swirling around Keely. Keely herself was a danger—to his peace of mind.

She was making him feel strange and vulnerable in some unfamiliar way. His pulse was racing for no good reason.

"I promise, no present," he said. "I'd like to come to dinner with you. Thank you."

Chapter 9

Primping. She was actually primping. And she was running late after a state trooper had stopped in at the store, finally, to take her statement. A forensics team had been called out of the city to take a look down at the farm and she'd be notified when the scene was cleared for her to attempt to salvage anything out of the pile that was left of her home. For now, it was a crime scene.

Her *home*, which, by the way, was demolished, was a crime scene. She could definitely use some distraction from that, and maybe it explained the primping.

Or maybe she was just kidding herself, bigtime. There was something peculiar happening inside her whenever she looked into Jake's eyes. She got the feeling she was seeing a soul that matched her own—a little wounded, a little protected, a little scared, pretending to the world and themselves that they didn't want or need anyone else. That thought drew her up short. She was in serious danger of getting stupid about him.

Keely put her brush down and stared at herself in the mirror. Her lipstick looked perfect now, but it'd be all gone with the first bite of food. Somehow Lise could eat an entire meal without so much as smudging her lips, but Keely hadn't been born with that gene.

She couldn't remember the last time she'd worn anything but jeans and a T-shirt, even to the small community church she'd attended all her life. Haven was on perpetual casual Friday dress code. It was just that kind of town. Country folk.

But she was wearing Lise's clothes tonight, a bundle Lise had brought over for her this morning since all her own clothes were buried under a pile of rubble at the farmhouse. Lise tended to be a bit dressier than most people in Haven. She had an image to maintain, the town manager's wife with political aims beyond the local scene.

Keely didn't worry too much about her image, but it was her birthday, right? She didn't turn thirty every day.

You get to start over.

Maybe Jake had been right. Maybe letting her anger out today had been good for her. Venting out loud to someone.

But what did she really know about him? She'd made bad judgments about men before. She'd told him a lot more about herself than he'd told her about him.

Her instincts, if she could trust them, told her he was a good person. Anyway, he was just a friend, so what did it matter? She had told her mother so quite firmly when she'd called earlier to let her know he was coming with her.

So why did this tiny voice inside her keep reminding her that the way she felt about him had nothing to do with friendship? She worked to block it out.

She wasn't really dressing up that much, just a soft, black halter top instead of a T-shirt, and she'd still put on jeans—jeans with embroidery across the rear. Lise was a few pounds lighter than her so they fit snug and she felt sexy. It was good to be thirty and feel sexy.

It was bad to be ridiculously excited about seeing Jake again.

She left the tiny bathroom and walked back into the studio-style apartment on the second floor of the store. The rest of the upstairs was devoted to a sort of antique-store-type room, huge and open, where local crafters sold goods on consignment along with whatever antiques Ray had supposedly collected from estate auctions. The inventory still made her uncomfortable, but she didn't know what to do about it.

There was no proof the items were hot. She'd stickered them at bargain basement prices after Ray's death and she donated the profit beyond what covered her living expenses to the church. She'd be glad when it was all gone.

The apartment was dusty and she hadn't had a chance to clean it with her time focused on straightening up the store, but she'd brought fresh sheets to put on the pullout sofa bed tonight. There was a mini-fridge in the pint-size kitchen that was really just a wall of countertop with a hot plate against one side of the apartment. The bachelor who'd owned the store before Ray bought it had lived in the apartment for years, so it was comfortable if spartan, all the necessities in place. A long-dead philodendron sat in the window that overlooked the road.

She missed the farmhouse.

Keely sat on the worn but serviceable sofa and stared out the window, across the road. There were lights on inside the rental house. It was a tiny, quaint, white clapboard home, perched near the road with a cliff dropping down behind it. She saw the front door of the house open, and Jake emerge.

She rose, looking back at the small marble-topped coffee table in front of the sofa. The box from Ray sat there.

What if it was connected to a murder? She couldn't believe that, or maybe didn't want to any more than she wanted to believe Ray had been involved in a murder at all. She didn't want to believe any of the events surrounding that skull she'd found.

Almost not wanting to touch it, she took the box from the table. The air in the room seemed to rush around her. Her vision swirled and her pulse rocked.

Her heart hammered painfully. She heard a *thunk* and realized she'd dropped the box. Her vision cleared and she felt as if some kind of energy sucked back from her, shaking her on her feet.

She blinked several times. She should have eaten lunch. She was hungry and tired and— She bent down, reached for the box. A shiver ran through her.

Picking up her purse, she quickly tucked the box inside. She didn't plan on opening it in front of her parents, but she didn't like leaving it just sitting here, either.

What was she going to do, though? Carry it around—for how long?

She was scared to open it, she confessed to herself. It was silly. If it proved to be some sort of evidence connected to the skull, she'd give it to the police. If it was just a guilt gift from a philandering husband to his wife, then she'd deal with that, too, and all the emotions it brought up. She knew she had to open it alone. She didn't want to listen to her family and friends putting down Ray while she was receiving a gift from him.

She'd end up defending him out of some sense of obligation, dammit, and she didn't want to defend him. Letting out that anger today *had* been good for her.

Downstairs, the store was still busy. Customers moved around the aisles, but up front the line of

people at the checkout stood still, heads all craned
to the TV over the counter, which was tuned to cable news. Tammy, ample and fortyish, had her fingers frozen over the register. Video footage of
Haven's main street stopped Keely short.

"The four-point-three shock wasn't all that took
rural residents of the small West Virginia county
by surprise last night," the female announcer
stated. "Panicked homeowners reported bursts of
horizontal light and a reddish haze in the air. Vol-
unteer fire trucks responded to a variety of loca-
tions, but found no flames to douse. One resident
called a paranormal detective after a four-year-
old boy was found, scratched and confused, along
a roadside this morning. The boy claimed to have
been trapped inside a red ball of light.

"What's behind all these strange reports? Is it
panic? Shara Shannon from PAI, the Paranormal
Activity Institute, is on the ground in Haven, the
epicenter of the quake, with town mayor Johnny
Southern."

Oh. My. God.

Keely couldn't believe her ears. She stood,
rooted, staring at the TV along with the other customers. She knew Johnny Southern wanted to ramp
up Haven's profile—turn the sleepy farmtown into

some kind of artsy-craftsy tourist mecca, taking advantage of its close proximity to the city. He'd been pumping his ambitious plan for years.

She wasn't against anything that would boost her own bottom line at the grocery store, but along with most residents, she didn't want to see Haven lose its small town charm.

Making the town sound like a loony bin wasn't charming. She hoped his appearance didn't mean he was willing to go that far.

"What's going on here in Haven, Mayor Southern?" the cable anchor asked. "Panic or paranormal activity? Some people have even suggested the possibility of UFOs in the area."

"An event like we had last night here in Haven takes everyone by surprise," the mayor said, his gravelly voice steady with a slight edge of nervousness. "Haven has never been known to have an earthquake. Emergency officials inside and outside the town are to be commended for their quick response and efficient clearing of roads and bridges. Volunteers have been out in droves today providing water and other necessities, particularly to our older residents. Most buildings received minimal damage and we plan on having the town back to normal as soon as possible."

"But things don't sound normal in Haven, Mayor Southern," the anchor pointed out. "What do you think is behind these bursts of horizontal light?"

Johnny Southern's expression remained noncommittal. *He doesn't know which way the wind is going to blow on this*, Keely thought. He's playing politics—happy to gain attention for himself and the town, reluctant to take a real stand till he knows how local residents are going to react.

"We did have a lightning storm last night, hitting right before the quake—" the mayor started.

"I believe I can answer that question," Shara Shannon, the PAI spokesperson, cut in. Her hair was a deep auburn, sleek, brushing the shoulders of her stylishly cut suit. She didn't look like a crazy person, but—

The bell over the door dinged.

"Let me start by saying that UFOs aren't behind what witnesses saw in the Haven area. Conditions last night, the low pressure and dense moisture, combined with an earthquake of that particular magnitude, form the 'perfect storm,' if you will, of atmospheric conditions to release positive ions into the air," Shara Shannon explained. "Positive ions trigger supernatural wavelengths, and those bursts of reddish light reported by residents are in line with what PAI has long tracked in other parts of the world as foundational movement."

"Foundational movement?"

"Yes. Foundational movement for oncoming paranormal activity."

"What type of paranormal activity can residents of Haven and the surrounding areas expect?"

Keely couldn't tell if the anchor was taking this interview seriously or not.

"Anything can happen in Haven now," Shara Shannon replied. Her eerily bright green eyes gazed directly into the camera. "And probably will."

Keely had the urge to roll her eyes but a sudden pounding headache stopped her. Or maybe it was the chill fingering down her spine. Shara Shannon was a nut. Nobody in their right mind would take her seriously.

"On that note, we're out of time, but please come back again, Ms. Shannon," the cable anchor said. "Our thanks as well to Haven mayor Johnny Southern."

A commercial flashed on, replacing Shara Shannon's perfectly groomed, seriously spooky face on the screen.

"I'm locking my doors tonight," one of the customers, an older lady with her hair up in a tight bun, said.

"People have been saying all day that they saw those lights," Tammy said.

"I didn't see nothing," a man in overalls put in.

A little girl, ice-cream cone dripping down her hand from the short-order counter at the back, leaned around her mother.

"What are positive tryons?"

"Ions," her mother said. "Positive ions. I don't know." She looked uneasy. "But I don't like it. I wonder if I should let you go to school tomorrow."

"Tammy." Keely nodded pointedly at the cash register. People were standing in line and the line wasn't moving. And she was afraid if they stood here much longer dwelling on that news interview, there was going to be a panic.

Earthquakes were rarely felt in West Virginia. The quake had turned everyone's world upside down by surprise and people were vulnerable. Even she had gotten a little shaky thinking about that flash of light right before the house had caved in on her. And the way that box had tumbled into her hand. But it was all explainable in the realm of reality.

"Okay, okay." Tammy got back to work.

Keely turned and all but bumped right into Jake Malloy's hard chest. She hadn't even realized he'd been in the store.

The chill inside her turned hot. Was that her heart thundering in her ears?

"Hi," she managed.

He was wearing the leather jacket again, this time over a white button-down shirt. He'd dressed for dinner, too, and looked more devastatingly handsome than ever. Even the most hardened of women would have to notice him. Small comfort.

"Ready to go?"

"My truck's not back. It *is* still at Dickie's, by the way." That had been a relief. It wasn't her truck that had busted out of the barn earlier. "Can we go in your car?"

"Sure."

She glanced back at Tammy, who unfortunately was not the most hardened of women and most definitely was noticing him along with the entire checkout line. Trouble with a small town was the gossip. She'd just become the center of some of that, she figured.

"I'm going to my folks' for dinner. Lock up, okay?" The store closed at nine and the way her family liked to talk, she didn't think she'd be back in time.

Outside, Jake turned to her.

"Did you hear from anyone about what you found out at the farm?"

She nodded. "A trooper came out and took my statement. You?"

"Yes. I was just wondering if you heard anything further."

"A forensics team will be handling the site. They're supposed to notify me when it's cleared so I can see if there's anything I can salvage from the rubble. I don't know anything else, like if the skull was still there, or more bones. I guess they'll let me know."

"Okay. Good."

She stopped on the edge of the road to take a look both ways, then tried not to notice the way Jake's palm lightly brushed her back as if watching out for her as they crossed the two-lane highway. It was an automatic gesture, chivalrous but meaningless. She liked it, though. Liked the feeling of his arm around her.

"I guess you saw all that about the paranormal stuff." She was making conversation, hoping the ball of nerves in her throat would go away. What was she, sixteen years old and afraid of being alone with a boy?

Not that Jake was anybody's idea of a boy. He was a man, tough as nails, but quietly kind despite first impressions. Her pulse raced with stupid nerves. This was no date and yet she felt like it was.

"Do you know what positive ions are?"

He shrugged. "Some kind of electrically charged particles."

"What did you think about all that?"

They'd reached his car parked in front of the rental house across the road. He had his hand on the door, set to open it for her.

"I think they need something to talk about when they carry news twenty-four hours a day." He shrugged. "Of course, anything's possible."

He'd surprised her. "You believe what that woman was saying from the Paranormal Activity Institute?"

"I didn't say that." He opened the door for her. Keely slid into the passenger seat of the economy-size lease car. "I just stopped thinking I knew it all a while back. Whenever you start thinking you know everything, that's when life hits you on the ass."

He shut the door and walked around the car to the driver's side and got in.

"Which way?" he asked when he'd keyed the engine.

She gave him directions as he pulled onto the highway. She watched his rock-hard profile, wondering about his comment.

"You get hit on the ass by life much?" she couldn't resist asking. He'd told her about his partner. That had to hurt, and maybe that was why he'd been sent away on R&R.

"Doesn't everybody?" His voice was even, giving nothing away.

"Not really. My friend Lise. She's married to her high-school sweetheart. Tom. Her life's pretty perfect, I'd say. She doesn't get hit on the ass much."

"It's good that you aren't jealous."

"I am not!" Dammit. "Well, okay, maybe a little bit."

Jake's mouth quirked and it was hard to be defensive. He wasn't judging her.

She turned her gaze from his profile to the narrow country road she'd directed him to turn onto off the highway. "I like my life. Mostly. Hers just seems a little simpler."

"Nobody's life is simple to them."

"I know." She looked back at Jake. "You like your life, Jake?"

"When I get one, I'll let you know," he said.

She felt a flush of embarrassment at how much *she'd* opened up to *him*. Obviously, it wasn't a two-way street.

"I thought we were friends." Jeez, she sounded pissy now and she hated that.

He shot her a look. "We *are* friends, Keely."

"Then tell me who you are. I don't mean your name, but *who you are*. Who is Jake Malloy?" She realized they were almost at their destination. "Turn there." She pointed to a fork in the road. "Then the first drive is my parents' house."

Jake made the turn then pulled down the drive and stopped behind a black SUV.

"Who is Jake Malloy? What do you want to know, Keely?" He gazed at her and she knew he was trying to decide how much to tell her. "I grew up in Charleston. My dad died in a crash ten years ago out in Pocahontas County, right after I graduated from WVU. My mom had cancer and passed a while back, too. They were divorced. She was married and divorced five times by the time I was out of high school."

"I'm sorry."

"That stuff, like most things you apologize for, isn't your fault."

"I know that. I'm just sorry you had to go through it."

"It's all right. I'm tough."

He gave her a cocky smile, as if he didn't have a care in the world. He was covering up, though. She could see the pain underneath. She knew all about covering up.

"What else do you want to know? I watch the History Channel and I like math. I count things."

"Count things?" Now he'd thrown her.

"To get stuff off my mind. I count things. Steps, passing cars, people, anything. I count at night. I used to count backward, but now I count forward because you run out of numbers the other way."

She remembered their conversation about trouble sleeping.

"Why are you in Haven on R & R?"

Silence stretched taut. There was no more cocky smile on his face. "They say I'm not dealing with my partner's death very well. I think I'm doing fine."

He didn't seem that fine to her. "You have trouble sleeping."

"So do lots of people."

That was true. She did, for example. But she didn't think it was quite the same. Or maybe it was…. "Do you feel guilty about his death?" She remembered that he'd said he'd saved the kid. He'd been too late to save his partner. "Do you think you did something wrong?"

"Nothing ever goes down perfect," he said. "I should have known that. The backup didn't get there in time. Brian's cover got blown. I wasn't there in time. I couldn't save him." His voice was hoarse suddenly.

"Maybe if you'd been there in time, you would have died, too," she pointed out gently. "Then you wouldn't have been able to save the child. You saved a child. That's a good thing. Brian would have wanted you to save the child first."

"He told me to get the girl. He told me to get her first."

"Then forgive yourself. I'm sure Brian does."

He was silent, his chiseled face in stark profile now. She could almost feel his pain, stretching across the short space between them in the shadows of the car. Seeing the way he blamed himself made her take another look at her own thought patterns.

"I felt responsible for Ray's death," she said quietly. "Still do sometimes. We had a fight right before he drove off that day. I felt like it was my fault that he did something that stupid, but it wasn't my fault. He did a lot of stupid things and none of them were my fault."

Jake looked back at her. "You're one of the nicest people I've ever met. Nothing you could have ever done justified how he treated you."

"I'm not all that nice."

He reached out, touched her face, skimmed his fingers along her jaw. "Yeah, you are. You're damn nice."

She saw all the pain and need she was feeling reflected back at her in his eyes. She understood him, too.

Quiet stretched between them.

"Why did you come here with me tonight?" she asked.

"Nothing else to do in this one-horse town, is there?" He added more seriously, "I'm worried about you. I'm worried that you're in danger."

He was worried about her. That was unbearably sweet. And dammit, she was wanting him again.

Her so-called friend.

Her stomach clenched. What was wrong with her? Why couldn't she keep this to a friendship? She didn't want a man in her life, especially one who clearly had no lasting interest in the community she adored. And she had plenty of problems, including a possible murder.

And yet...

Yeah, she was in danger, but not the kind Jake meant.

Chapter 10

The front door of the house opened.

"I think we've been made," he said. "Ready?"

She looked oddly reluctant to go inside, and he wasn't all that eager himself.

"I think I should tell you something," Keely said. She put her hand on his arm, stopped him before he could get out of the car. "The people who love me are hell-bent on setting me up. That's what the wart thing was about."

"Wart thing?" He vaguely recalled her friend making mention of something along those lines.

"Lise was bugging me. Wanted to know all about you. I told her you were old and fat and had a wart."

He had to laugh. "Thanks."

"Sorry." She blushed.

"It's too late for me to grow one," he said, working to keep things light. "Or get fat and old."

"That's okay." She laughed now, too, and he could see the tension break in her eyes. "I'm just letting you know so that you'll be prepared. They won't be content with your being my friend. We'll just have to be firm about it, and you might have to be a little patient with their pushiness. They're good people."

He hoped she was right. A large, rugged-looking man was heading down the steps from the front of the house. Jake and Keely met him halfway and Jake reached out to shake the hand offered to him. The older man's grip was firm, his gaze level. He wore crisp slacks and a golf shirt, casual yet clean-cut.

"Dad, this is Jake Malloy."

"Howard Bennett," he introduced himself. "I want to thank you for being there with our Keely last night when the quake hit. She told us you were a big help to her. Good to meet you."

"It's good to meet you, too, but I didn't really do anything," Jake responded.

"Just being there was important to her," Howard argued. "And important to us."

"We're so glad to have you here. Roxie, Keely's mother." The woman who came up behind Howard Bennett was petite, much slighter than Keely's tall build. "I'm just thrilled that you're having dinner with us."

Both of her parents were regarding him with obvious interest. They both seemed young and physically fit for their age. Roxie Bennett was attractive, her slender face carefully made up, looked younger than her years.

"Thank you, Mrs. Bennett."

"No, now you just call me Roxie."

Howard slapped an affable arm around Jake's back and guided him into the house. It smelled like fried chicken and fresh baked bread inside and his mouth watered just a little. It'd been a long time since he'd had home cooking. A long time since he'd been part of any kind of family gathering.

He looked back for Keely. Her mother seemed to be fussing over her, but he couldn't hear what they were saying as they entered the house to the sound of a baby's wail.

A woman walked into the airy foyer of the home, a chubby baby dressed in a sailor suit draped over one shoulder.

"Hi there," she said over the child's crying. She jiggled the boy on her shoulder and he quieted to a sobbing hiccup. "Paul, come meet Keely's friend," she called over her shoulder. "I'm Sherry, Keely's brother's wife."

She positively beamed at Jake.

A man appeared behind her, another sailor-suited baby in his arms. "I'm Paul." He shook Jake's hand while cradling the baby in his other arm. He was tall and bore a striking resemblance to his father.

More people than he could imagine fitting into the house started filling the foyer, all with curious looks at him while calling birthday greetings to Keely. She'd been just about swamped in hugs. He learned that Keely had two brothers, as well as a sister. There were several cousins and friends, with children and spouses.

"Danny, hey, thanks for coming," Keely was saying as she stepped around him, brushing against him in the press of family and friends. She gave the man who was as big as a linebacker a warm hug, then said, "Where's Mary?"

"Out back with the kids," Danny said.

"Mary's a good friend of mine," Keely explained. "This is her husband, Danny. He teaches at the high school and coaches football."

"Now let's not crowd in here when we've got a whole house," Roxie Bennett said, shooing everyone back into the living room. The furnishings were comfortable, informal cottage-style with lots of florals and checks. Jake went with the flow as they spilled out onto a spacious back deck where he saw at least one person he recognized—Lise Tanner.

"You came! I'm so glad," Lise welcomed him. "Meet my husband, Tom."

Premature sparks of silver at his temples, wire-rimmed eyeglasses and a slender frame gave Tom Tanner an academic air. He reached his hand out to grip Jake's, then turned to Keely. "Happy birthday. Some birthday, eh?"

Keely's friend Mary, he discovered, was the woman in the flowing purple-patterned summer dress with beads draped around her neck and a couple of kids hanging onto her ankles.

He thought about his own family and old friends, split up about a hundred different ways. He had some stepsiblings from his mother's later marriages. He wasn't close to any of them and hadn't been in touch with old school friends in years. Haven was the kind of place where people grew up and stayed together. It was all foreign to him.

"Sit down, sit down. Now. Tell us about yourself," Roxie invited as she sat down on a padded redwood chair across from Jake, who found himself shooed to a seat next to Keely. There was a stack of beautifully wrapped birthday gifts on the umbrella-topped outdoor dining table. This crowd wasn't going to fit around it but he could see that there were plenty of seats, some nice redwood and other extra plastic chairs that had probably been brought out for the occasion. Flowers overflowed from pots and wind chimes hung from poles on the ends of the deck.

Keely had one of the bouncing baby boys on her lap. One of her cousin's daughters was running laps around a bird feeder in the smoothly cut sloping lawn that stretched to a line of trees. The sun had dipped below the trees and shadows crossed the lawn. A chorus of cicadas beat the crisp, clear air.

"What brings you to Haven?" Roxie prompted when Jake didn't reply right away.

Keely's gaze slid from the giggling baby to Jake. She looked gorgeous with a baby, he thought unexpectedly. She also looked extremely curious, waiting for his response.

"Country living," he came up with. "Peace and quiet." It was true enough, though not his idea.

That brought a laugh from Keely's father. "And we greet you with an earthquake and a media frenzy. What kind of work do you do?"

"I'm not working right now."

"I could help you find some work if you like," Tom put in. "I work for the town."

Well, Jake had managed to give the impression that he was out of work and slightly better than a bum. He figured that would help Keely out with the matchmaking problem.

"Tom helps everybody," Lise put in. "You should see him at Christmas. We hardly even see him because he's out buying food and presents for the families of everybody who comes through the local shelter."

"Girls, would you help me in the kitchen?" Roxie asked, and Keely's sister, sisters-in-law and friends exited, one of them with her arm swung happily around Keely's shoulders.

The people who love me... Yep, she had a lot of people who loved her, that was clear. He wondered if they were all really as nice as they seemed. Or maybe that was just his suspicious, bitter-cop side coming out.

He found himself hoping they were all as nice as they seemed. The scene before him was like some fantasy family gathering. He didn't fit in, didn't belong.

Keely's mother was no doubt dragging Keely off to point out how unsuitable he was as husband material, bringing along the rest of the women for added support. And he *was* unsuitable, just not for the reasons Keely's family knew about. Her friend Mary was the last to go, grabbing up the lap-running three-year-old from the lawn on her way. Another little girl, maybe six, ran behind her. Sherry had left the twin babies with her husband, who looked somewhat pained as he attempted to juggle the two of them.

"You all live around here?" Jake asked Tom and Danny, who were both seated near him.

Danny took another beer out of a big cooler on the deck and offered one to Jake. "We've got a place out on Black Hollow Road," Danny said. "It'd take a forklift for me to get Mary out of Haven. When we have kids, she wants to raise them here, where she grew up."

"We're out on Lick Fork," Tom said. "Just built a new house last year."

The town manager was doing pretty good, Jake guessed as he opened his beer. Keely's parents were doing all right, too, judging by the nice home he'd passed through on his way to the deck. It was well-furnished, comfortable, very modern and full of light. Nothing like Keely's farmhouse, he thought as the men's conversation turned to the disaster.

"It's too bad about what happened to the old family farmhouse," Jake said.

"Hopefully we can salvage something out of it," Howard said. "It's a huge loss, in terms of family treasures, but—"

"Maybe Keely can move on now," Tom said. "We tried to talk her out of living out there when Ray died. I never thought she was safe there by herself. And now, with what she says she found—"

"I went out there today to get something out of my car," Jake said casually. "My car got hit by a tree in the storm, right before the shock hit. Someone'd been tampering with the site before the police got there. The dirt was freshly turned out behind the house and someone rammed a white pickup truck out of the barn, blew the doors down, nearly ran me over."

He'd taken careful note of the vehicles in the driveway and parked in the yard when he'd driven up. None of them had been white pickups. Of course, there he went, being paranoid and suspicious again.

"Now that worries me," Howard said. "I don't want Keely out there at all."

"I agree," another of her brothers—David? Jake couldn't remember his name—added.

"I'm just wondering who knew about what she found," Jake said.

"Unfortunately, probably a lot of people," Tom said. "I heard about it this afternoon from my secretary, who'd had lunch with one of the dispatchers. Of course, she knew it was my sister-in-law in this case, but people talk. They shouldn't, but they do, and finding a skull in your rose bed is certainly good gossip around here. We don't get a lot of murders in Haven. But for all we know, might not be human bones. Could just be animal bones."

"Keely said she saw a human skull."

"You know she probably took off screaming the second her shovel hit it," Danny said jokingly. "You know how women are. Could've just been another animal digging around since she'd uncovered bones."

"I still don't like the sound of this whole thing," Howard said. "I'd rather Keely was staying here now."

"I don't think we need to overreact until we have more information," Tom said. "Let the police do their job."

Lise popped her head out of the kitchen. "Tom! Phone." She spoke over her shoulder to her husband as he headed past her to the phone inside. "Do *not* give him any money! It's Jud Peterson again. I'm tired of his freeloading and now he's tracking you over here, for Pete's sake. Used to, he'd at least do a half-ass drunken odd job for a few dollars but now he just wants handouts." Tom was already gone with the phone. She turned to Howard. "Tom is such an easy touch. We've got a new house and bills to pay and he's financing Jud Peterson's binges. Anyway, dinner's ready."

Done venting, she disappeared in a huff.

"Come on, Jake, don't be shy," Roxie called from the dining table. "There's plenty, so eat up," she went on as Jake lined up where directed and picked up a plate. The crowd filled the dining room and one by one they carried full plates outside. Everyone seemed to talk at once.

"We've got spice cake with whipped cream

frosting, Keely's favorite, for dessert," Roxie said, "and then we'll open presents."

"Have you opened that present from Ray?" Lise asked Keely as she sat down next to Jake in one of the plastic chairs.

"No."

Tom came back out to the deck with his plate, having finished his phone conversation. Jake noticed Lise gave him the cold shoulder when he sat down beside her.

Roxie did a double take. "What present from Ray?"

"It's nothing," Keely said. "I found a little box, all wrapped up, with happy birthday written on it, from Ray. I'll open it when I'm ready. I don't want to talk about it."

"Okay, honey." Roxie Bennett's fork froze over her mashed potatoes for a beat before she went on, turning to Jake. "Keely says you two are just friends."

Keely didn't look any happier with this topic. "Mom—"

"Good plan," Mary quipped to Jake. "She's shy. You don't want to scare her off."

Keely seemed focused on her plate, determined to ignore her family.

"Why don't you join us at church on Sunday?"

Roxie invited Jake. "It's the Haven Community Church on the main highway west of town."

"I bet Tom can get you a line on some work," Lise said. "With the damage in the county, there's going to be a lot of reconstruction. You look like you could handle a hammer."

What was he now, a charity project?

"People really don't need to wait a year after they're widowed to start dating," Roxie said. "I keep telling Keely that went out of style a long time ago. It's fine."

"Especially since Ray was such a cheating, lying bastard," Lise added.

Keely's jaw tightened. "We're not dating."

Mary's head swiveled to her friend. "Then why did you sleep with him?"

Keely went beet-red.

The whole deck went silent. A bird chirped in the woods.

Mary clapped her hand over her mouth. "Oh my God," she breathed into the charged air. "I really am psychic."

"That went well."

Jake backed the car up the dark driveway. Keely didn't respond for a moment. She felt shy and embarrassed, and the even-keeled way he'd dealt with everything from the earthquake to dinner made her both more attracted and more scared.

"I'm sorry. That was awkward for you. I don't know what made Mary say that. I never said anything to make her think that. Thank God everyone seemed to take my word for it that she was wrong. She's not psychic, you know. She does this palm-reading and tarot card thing, mostly at local carnivals, sometimes out of her house, private readings. But even she doesn't take it seriously. It's her home business, she calls it."

"It's okay. Don't worry about it."

"Thanks. No wonder my family likes you." How could they help liking him? "They don't even care that you made it sound as if you were out of work." *Hot*, that's what Mary had called him.

"I tried to help you out," Jake said, sliding her a grin she could barely make out in the lights from the dash. The night was dark and still. Electricity was back on tonight in most of the county and as they drove, lights twinkled from the occasional farmhouse.

They reached the highway and headed into Haven proper. Businesses were closed except for the small gas station. The community building was dark, whatever emergencies remained being shuttled up for care at the hospital. The peak of the crisis had passed. Haven could return to normal now. The Foodway was dark inside, the lighted sign illuminating the front.

"Thank you," Keely said as Jake pulled up in front of the store. She gathered up the bag of presents she'd brought back—some new and now desperately needed clothes, some of the homemade candles her sister made, some pottery she'd admired at the fair in Cedar Lakes last year when she'd gone with her mother.

"I could walk up with you, make sure everything's all right." Jake regarded her seriously. "I'm worried."

"You don't need to be. I'll be fine." If she couldn't even walk into her apartment without someone holding her hand, she was going to have a hard time getting through the rest of her life. "Maybe Tom is right and all I saw were animal bones."

The intensity in his look didn't flinch. "I'll wait out here until I know you're inside and everything's okay."

"Whatever you want to do." She frowned. "That didn't come out right. I appreciate your concern. I just don't want to be a bother."

"You're not a bother. I'm your friend, remember?"

She avoided his gaze by staring at his shoulders in the darkened car. He had very broad shoulders. His arms had felt so good wrapped around her last night when she'd been scared. She couldn't look at Jake Malloy without him arousing tender, hungry feelings that had no place in her life. He made her think of the type of man she'd wished she'd married. Someone not at all like Ray.

"Then I'm just bothering myself," she said and pushed the car door open. "Maybe I don't know how to be your friend."

Oh, damn. Now she'd gone and said something more stupid than ever.

"Hey—"

"Good night." She wrestled with her purse, thank God finding her keys immediately, and was in the door and had it shut behind her before Jake could think twice about coming after her. If he was thinking about coming after her. He was probably starting to think she belonged in an asylum the way she ran hot and cold on him.

If she wasn't confusing him, she was definitely confusing herself.

Night-lights lent enough illumination for her to find the stairs that led to the apartment and antique/consignment shop. She unlocked the apartment and reached for the switch beside the door.

She never knew what hit her.

Chapter 11

Jake leaned against the car, the engine turned off, waiting to see the light flick on inside the upstairs apartment. Movement from inside the darkened store caught the corner of his eye. A shadowy blur raced through the store, knocking down a display near the register, heading for the back.

A blur that was way too big to be Keely.

His heart kicked into overdrive. He leaped the few steps to the front of the store. Locked! He rattled the door then banged on it, swore roundly and raced for the back, toward where he'd seen the shadow heading. He reached for his gun as he tore through the pitch-black around the side of the building.

Keely. Dammit, if anything had happened to her— The rush of emotion was so fierce, it nearly stopped him. He charged on, pushing away the mindblowing fear he felt for her.

He heard a crash from the back of the building as he reached it and a shadow dashed between two Dumpsters, heading for a high chain-link fence. Breath seared Jake's lungs as he leaped, grappling at—

Air.

A thud from the other side of the fence told him he'd been too late. The shadow was gone, in a split second, into the trees behind the store. And he could either chase after him, and most likely lose him in the twist of residential streets and woods that whoever the hell that had been probably knew way better than Jake did, or he could find Keely—

There was no second thought to that one.

He whipped around, raced for the open rear door of the store. He found himself in the kitchen, stumbling against what he realized was a stove. The short-order kitchen.

The store was dark, dimly lit by low night lights near the front counter.

"Keely?" he shouted, hoarse from running, as he tore up the stairs to where he knew the apartment would be. It was even darker here. No light at all. He found a doorway, open, and reached for what he hoped would be a light switch—

Bright light from an overhead fixture temporarily blinded him. Then he saw her.

Soft, tangled hair. She lay on the floor, still. Blood pounded in his veins. He didn't even feel his feet move the steps it took to reach her.

"Keely." He bent down, pushed the hair from her face. There was no blood that he could see, but she was so still—"Keely!"

Her lashes fluttered. His heart nearly exploded in his chest. She blinked, her eyes dark in her pale, shell-shocked face. She stared at him for an agonizing beat, as if trying to figure out what had just happened.

"Someone was in my apartment," she whispered raggedly. "They hit me. Oh, God." She pushed up on her elbows, slowly, painfully, edged backward, struck the edge of a coffee table.

"He's gone. I saw him run through the store. I went after him, saw him run out of the back of the store."

Dammit, he wished he hadn't lost him. Whoever had done this to Keely, he could kill him with his bare hands right now. He wouldn't need a gun.

"Are you all right?"

She didn't look all right. She looked terrified, and she'd been hit. He could see a bruise blooming on her temple.

"He slammed me to the floor. I think. How long was I out? I don't understand what happened." She sounded so confused, it hurt to hear her speak.

"Just a few minutes."

"How could he have gotten in? Everything was locked."

"The back door was open, through the kitchen. Either he had a key, or he broke in, or someone left it unlocked. I'm calling the police."

He saw a phone on an end table and grabbed for it, punched 911 as he went back to Keely. He wasn't leaving her side. He made the report quickly then put the phone down. Her quiet devastation broke what was left of his restraint. He placed his hand on her head, stroked the tangled hair there.

Thank God. Thank God she was alive.

"They'll be here soon," he said. "And I'm not leaving."

Sobs shook her suddenly, and there was no

question in his mind. He wrapped his arms around her, just held her. She'd wanted him to go away a few minutes before, when she'd gotten out of his car, but she wasn't asking him to go away now.

She burrowed her face into his shirt and the urge to pull her even closer blindsided him. She was shaking and he realized he was, too.

"Thank you," she choked out through tears. "Thank you for watching out for me."

His chest wound tighter. "I told you it wasn't a bother. I'm not going to let anyone hurt you." He meant it. He wasn't going to let any arm come to her, not if he could help it.

She lifted her face to him, her mouth a mere whisper away, and he moved, just so, and touched his lips to hers. She made a sound in her throat, needy, aching, and he forgot all about self-discipline. He kissed her, needing to taste her, hot and sweet and alive. And she was responding. She wanted him just as he wanted her.

He shifted his weight, nestling her closer against him, kissing her deeper. She pushed herself snugly against him and he knew this was a mistake, a bad, bad mistake. She wasn't a one-night-stand woman, he knew that, and two nights wouldn't make it any more right. He'd leave Haven before long and she'd be left with a broken heart.

Pulling back, he stared down at her, desperate need fighting with his better sense.

"I don't want to hurt you," he said, low, fierce. "I don't want to take advantage of you. I'm sorry."

Keely held Jake's gaze, wishing— Oh, God, she was wishing for more. Wishing for last night all over again. And he was afraid he was taking advantage of her. He didn't really want her, not beyond a physical intersection between their two lives, what they'd had last night in the farmhouse. It was abundantly clear.

"You're not taking advantage of me." She tipped her chin, pain shooting through her temples at the movement. "It's no big deal. You don't have to explain." He'd just been comforting her, that was all.

"Just…don't go anywhere yet." She sounded pathetic and she hated that.

"I'm not going anywhere."

She blinked, swallowed hard over the lump of uncomfortable, confused emotion in her throat. What she really wanted was for him to hold her again and never let go. What happened to never wanting a man in her life again? Yeah, that had always been a lie.

She was just the cowardly lion, like always. Afraid just because Ray had been a bastard she'd never do any better, so she'd stuck with him, and once he was gone, she'd figured she'd rather be alone than risk getting hurt again.

It wasn't what she really wanted. Not if she had any guts.

"Maybe I should see if anything was taken." Yeah, that would keep her occupied, she thought desperately. She started going over the apartment.

"If they were here to steal, why would they be up here when there is a store full of anything they could want right down the stairs?" Jake asked.

She looked back him. His gaze was unreadable, dark. If he was as moved as she by that kiss, he wasn't showing it.

"They wanted something from you, Keely."

She shivered, froze.

"What?"

"The present from Ray?" he suggested. "It's just a thought. Where is it?"

Her purse. It was there, by the door, where she must have dropped it.

"It's in my purse. Maybe they didn't even see it. I was carrying that bag of stuff with me." The presents were scattered and she saw the pottery her mother had given her—in pieces on the floor. "Aw, hell."

Emotion welled up again. She didn't care that much about the pottery even though she'd admired it at the fair. It was just—

Everything. She was losing everything lately.

Even things she'd never had. Like Jake.

"They were probably in a rush to get out of here when you came in," Jake theorized. "But what else could they have been after?"

"I don't know." She blinked harder, willing back the tears that kept threatening.

The phone rang. She hurried toward it, pressed a hand to her temples as pain seared her head again. She grabbed the phone.

"Hello."

"Hey. I just wanted to apologize again."

"It's okay, Mary."

"It's not okay. I can't believe I said that in front of your whole family! I don't know where it came from. It just burst out of me. I feel terrible. I just want you to know that."

"It's okay. Really. It's okay."

Her friend was silent for a beat. "Are you okay? I keep having this awful feeling. I don't like this. I don't like these feelings I'm getting about you. I really don't want to know anything! I swear to God, I liked being a fake psychic. You *are* sleeping with that guy, aren't you?"

"Mary…" She didn't want to have this conversation. Usually, she told Mary almost everything, but she was too tired right now. "Someone broke in. There was an intruder in my apartment when I got back to the store. I have to go. The police are on the way."

That distracted Mary.

"Oh, no! What happened?"

"I walked in and someone knocked me out. That's all I know. Jake was here. He'd just dropped me off. He tried to chase after him but he lost him."

"Is he still there? You shouldn't be alone."

"Yes, he's here." She turned, saw Jake still standing there, looking so dangerous and protective all at once. "I'll be fine."

"Are you sure? Are you all right? Maybe you have a concussion. Maybe—"

"I'm okay, I promise."

"You shouldn't stay there by yourself tonight. I can come get you."

"No, don't do that. I'll figure something out. If I need someone I'll call you back. Okay?" There was a sound from the front of the store, downstairs. "I think the police are here. I have to go."

"I'll let them in, if you'll get me the key to the front," Jake said.

She took her purse and got out the key. Her knees felt wobbly and she was grateful for the help. In a minute, he was back with a uniformed trooper, the same trooper who'd come out to the store earlier to take her statement about the skull in her garden.

Briefly, Jake explained about the shadow figure he'd chased, and the trooper asked Keely if anything was missing. She hadn't had time to look around much, but she did now while the officer watched. She hadn't brought much personal to the apartment so far. If anything was missing that had been here before, she had no way of knowing.

"I had a bag of gifts with me," she said, pointing to the mess on the floor. "And my purse. But he didn't take any of that."

"Looks like you took him by surprise and he just wanted to get away," the trooper surmised. "I'll need a list of everyone who has a key to the building. I'll take some prints here, then down-stairs at the back. We'll see what we can find out behind the building where you saw someone." He looked at Jake then back to Keely. "He's long gone by now, I'm sure."

"What about my farm?" Keely asked. "Have you heard anything about that, about the skull I found?"

The officer nodded. "I was about to get to that. The forensics team didn't find anything, but I called in a few favors so they're going to keep working on it. They haven't cleared the site yet, so they're asking you not to go out and work on salvaging anything from the house yet. But so far, nothing."

"The skull was right there. I hit it with my shovel. It was uncovered." She felt, and sounded, panicked. She had seen a skull, she knew she had. "Couldn't they see that the scene had been disturbed?"

"They didn't see it before, ma'am, so they really can't tell," the trooper pointed out. "There was a lot of activity out there this morning, too. It might not have been disturbed by anyone on purpose. We just don't know right now."

Jake's gaze tightened. "I was out there this morning and saw the earth freshly turned, as if someone had been digging this afternoon. That was before the forensics people were out there and after the rescue team had left. And you know someone was out there. They tried to run me down."

"We just don't know," the trooper repeated. "It

could have been something that happened this morning—during the rescue operation. There were a lot of people out there. And we don't know who was out there or why they were out there. Might have had nothing to do with what Ms. Schiffer saw. Someone could have been there trying to take something from the rubble. If we had a plate number—"

"It happened too fast," Jake said. "But the soil was damp. The sun was hot yesterday—the soil would have been dried if it had been something that had been disturbed in the morning. I think whoever broke in here could have been looking for the box Keely's husband left her."

"What box?"

"A birthday present," Keely explained. "I guess we were thinking maybe it was connected to the murder." A tingle of fear rippled up her spine.

The trooper shook his head. "We don't have a murder yet."

"Someone took the skull," Jake said.

The trooper stared at him. "As I said, they haven't cleared the site yet, but they haven't found anything." He looked back at Keely. "Even if they do, we'd be a long way from connecting your husband to it, though we'd certainly start there. I don't know what we could do with your box at this point."

"Investigate?" Jake suggested.

She could see the frustration in the rigid set of his jaw. She was frustrated, too. She felt helpless and she was tired of feeling like her life was out of control.

"Here." She dug the box out of her purse and handed it to the trooper. Nerves jangled up her spine and the box felt cold in her hand. She was glad to drop it into his. "Why don't you open it and see what it is."

The trooper took the box. He tore the wrapping and pulled off the lid.

"It's a necklace," he said. "Just a necklace."

He tilted the box so she could see. A silver-and-garnet-encrusted heart lay inside, a long chain tangled beneath it.

"I don't see what we can make of this," the officer said. "I don't have a murder. I don't have a case to file evidence on. It looks like a gift to me."

It looked like a gift to her, too. She felt silly suddenly. And yet… Someone had broken in here tonight for something. If it wasn't the box from Ray, then what was it?

"If you'll make me that list while I get prints," he said, "I'll get out of your way."

She looked around for some paper and a pen.

Her head hurt and she resisted letting out her frustration on the trooper. He was doing his job as he saw it. She just didn't like the feeling that no one was taking her seriously about what she'd found in the garden. No one but Jake.

He was right about one thing, at least—if someone was out there to get that skull, then Ray hadn't acted alone in whatever was going on. And maybe that person had been right here in her apartment tonight.

Or maybe she'd imagined that skull had been human and the whole thing was nonsense. She didn't think so, but she was so confused, she didn't know what to think anymore.

The officer went around the apartment taking prints, then downstairs. When he came back, he took the list of employees with keys.

"I'll give you a call if anything turns up with the prints," he said. "And I'll let you know when the site is cleared out on your farm."

Jake followed the officer downstairs. She could hear the sound of the bolt sliding back, the key turning in the lock.

His tall, broad-shouldered frame filled the doorway of the apartment again. She met his gaze across the room.

"You're not staying here alone tonight," he said. "In fact, you shouldn't stay here at all. They might come back."

That wasn't a comforting thought. She was pretty much over the independent attitude with which she'd turned down Jake's offer to walk her upstairs earlier.

"I could go to my parents' or Lise's or Mary's...."

But then she might be bringing danger to their door, she thought with a sick, hollow dread in her stomach. Fear rippled through her. She wanted Jake to hold her again, but she was scared of that, too. He was a stranger. How could he be the one she wanted to run to for security? She felt like her life had become some kind of creepy roller-coaster ride in the dark and she didn't know when, or if the next frightening drop would occur.

She just knew that if it did, she wanted him to be the one seated next to her when she screamed.

His hard, comforting gaze seared right through her, as if he knew what she was thinking.

"I think you should stay with me," he said.

Chapter 12

"It's gonna rain again." The air was heavy, damp. The night stirred with a soft breeze and Keely shivered as she turned after locking up the store. "I love rain." Her expression was painfully wistful.

Jake guessed she was thinking about her normal life, the one she didn't have anymore.

"Yeah," he agreed. "I think it's gonna rain. Come on." He left his rental car parked in front of the store and they walked across the road even as the first splashes of the oncoming storm hit them.

Maybe someone was watching them. He wasn't

sure that they were that much safer across the road than they were at the store except that there was a good chance whoever had gotten in the store had gotten in with a key. At least at his rental house, they'd have to break in, make some racket.

He'd be ready if they did.

Inside the house, he flipped the switch by the door that turned on a lamp in the front room. Keely was quiet, her expression exhausted and troubled. He didn't know what to do to make her feel better. She sat on the brown-and-red-checked couch, seeming to try to make herself as small as possible. The house was simply decorated, comfortable, with cozy cream walls and serviceable furniture. An antique German clock ticked softly from across the room.

"Nobody believes me about the skull I saw," she said quietly.

"I believe you."

He saw the flare of fear in her eyes and he wished he could do something to take that fear away. He hated to scare her more, but she needed to see the reality of her situation.

"Someone put that skull in your garden. Last fall, we can guess, if that's when the old shrubs were torn out. And most likely Ray was involved. What was going on last fall, before he died?"

She turned her hollowed gaze to him. "He'd had a string of affairs. The women— I know their names, well, the ones I know about, I guess. There could be others for all I know." She looked away, at her hands fisted in her lap. "Otherwise, I don't know. He'd bought the store last year and we both worked there. Nobody's gone missing around here lately that I know of."

"We don't know when the murder took place."

Her gaze rose to him again. "But it couldn't have been any longer ago than last fall."

"Unless the body was being moved. But you only saw a skull, right?"

She nodded. It was possible that more of the skeleton could have been buried than she'd uncovered, or someone had only moved the skull. Maybe by tomorrow the forensics team would dig deeper and find further evidence out at the farm.

He watched as Keely opened her purse and pulled out the small box. She set it on the coffee table in front of her as if she didn't like touching it.

"I guess they weren't after this," she said. "It's just a necklace."

She lifted the lid again. The silver heart inlaid with garnets gleamed in the low lamplight from its nest inside the box. It was a necklace, just a necklace.

Keely didn't move to pick it up.

The air in the room remained taut somehow.

"It's just a necklace," she repeated finally, low. "It looks kind of old. There's a little tarnish on it. Maybe he got it on one of his antiquing forays."

"Maybe." There were other possibilities, including a link to murder. There was no proof of it, but he wasn't excluding the idea yet.

"I feel silly," Keely said. "Really, I think this whole situation has made me a little nuts. I think the whole town is going a little nuts. Positive ions. Flashing lights. Earlier, when I picked up the box, I felt…" She looked up at Jake. "I felt strange, like this weird rush of air." She gave a forced laugh. "The power of suggestion, you know? I mean, I think I was just hungry, feeling a little faint. Look at Mary. She thinks she's really psychic now."

None of that explained the skull she'd seen in her rose bed, though. That was before the quake. He didn't think Keely was the type of person to be swept up in a paranormal hysteria, either.

"None of this makes sense, that's all," she said. "And I don't like it." She shivered again, visibly. "I'm cold," she said. "I'm really, really cold. I just want to go to sleep."

"You can use my bed." There was only one

bedroom in the little rental house. It wasn't more than eight hundred square feet total, just the bedroom, kitchen, front parlor and bathroom.

"No. I'll take the couch. You're paying me to rent this house. I'm not taking your bed."

He wanted to argue with her, but he could see her obstinate exhaustion. Her shining eyes stabbed him.

"I'll get you a blanket." He went to the bedroom, pulled the blanket from the bed, along with a pillow, and brought them out to her. "I'd rather you took the bed," he said. "But you can do what you want."

"I'd feel better about it this way." She took the blanket and wrapped it around herself. She was pale and he could still see her shaking.

The temperature in the house couldn't be below seventy-five. There was no air-conditioning in the house, and the spring night was cool, but not *that* cool.

He didn't want to leave her alone, and he had no intention of sleeping. She needed sleep, though. She looked almost sick. He wanted to do something, but he felt helpless.

"I'll be in the kitchen, if you need me," he told her. "I'll turn on the heat. I can fix you some coffee, if you like." He'd picked up a few things before he'd left the store earlier.

She shook her head. "I just need to get some sleep." She put her head down on the couch, stretching her legs.

Outside, he could hear rain, steady now. He felt the pull of her, the desire inside him to find a way to comfort her and make her feel safe.

The best thing he could do for her, and himself, was to let her sleep.

He adjusted the thermostat, turned off the lamp and headed for the kitchen. He sat down at the laptop he'd brought with him and opened it. Connecting to the Internet, he did a search for the local newspaper. Six months ago, Ray had dug up a rose bed and now there was a skull in it. Something happened six months ago—either the murder itself, or the location change of the body. That was the theory he was going on.

He hunched over the screen, tapping through articles. Crime was low in Haven. No reports of missing persons. No murders. A few domestic violence reports, a suspicious fire, a case of animal neglect, minor burglaries, drug possession charges... He searched other news stories. Controversy over an iron bridge that needed repair or replacement, local elections, youth sports reports, a cancer run, a baby beauty contest, 4-H meetings...

He would have thought life in a small town would have put him to sleep, but an unfamiliar tug gnawed at him as he scanned the stories.

The simple life. It was oddly appealing.

The stray thought took him by surprise. So far, Haven had been quite a few letters short of heaven. He should hate Haven at this point and he sure as hell had no business even thinking about feelings of attachment to either Haven *or* Keely.

Detach. Focus.

The edgy feeling he'd had before came back. He didn't feel right in his own skin anymore.

Pushing aside the uncomfortable train of thought, he clicked on the next story. A two-hundred-acre abandoned farm the town had tried to buy. Tom Tanner had fought hard to convince the town to fork over the funds needed to purchase the land for use as a nature preserve. A developer had sneaked in under the wire and bought it out from under the town's nose with a higher bid. Flipping forward in time, he found that construction on a small subdivision of midpriced homes was underway.

His nape tingled. Reason to move a body?

It was a possibility, but there was certainly no evidence to suggest he was doing anything other than wildly speculating.

The site had a search function. He searched on missing persons, and came up with an Alzheimer's patient who'd wandered off, a few small children, a runaway—all found alive. A sixty-year-old local businessman had disappeared and been found dead, the killer apprehended and sent to prison. Nothing he could connect up to what Keely had uncovered back at her farm.

He pushed back from the table and started to walk toward the front room to check on Keely. Then he started running.

She was screaming.

Raging wind. Cold. Lights. Lights in the dark, roaring straight for her. She couldn't run fast enough. White light cut a swath right through her. Run! Terrified, she stumbled, hit hard—

"Keely!"

"No!"

"Keely! I'm not going to hurt you."

Gentle arms cradled her, holding her down. She'd hit him. She'd hit— Jake.

Her head reeled. She blinked, awareness coming at her in sickening increments. She still half felt as if she were somewhere else.

Someone else.

Where had that thought come from?

"I won't hurt you, I promise. Shh." He whispered to her, rocking her against his solid, warm body.

She was cold, so cold.

"I was—" She struggled to get the words out, her teeth chattering. "I had a bad dream?" She didn't mean it to be a question but she heard the confusion in her own voice. She struggled to focus on her surroundings, on reality. The dream had seemed so real….

"It's okay now. I'm here and I'm not going anywhere, I promise. You're okay. You fell off the couch."

She felt her heart pounding violently. Jake shifted and she gripped his shoulders, afraid he'd leave her. His gaze on her was deep, unwavering, shockingly patient, and she told herself to stop panicking. He wasn't going to leave her, he'd promised.

Promised. She hated promises, but she believed his. That was scarier than her dream.

He held her tighter. She was scared. He was comforting her. But that had nothing to do with the dangerous need causing her to practically climb up his body.

"Tell me about your dream," he said softly, still rocking her. "Tell me."

"I don't know." Already, the dream was disintegrating in her mind, disjointed images fading in and out. "It was like I was on a road. I think it was a road. I fell and it was hard. Lights were coming at me, like a car."

"You were afraid you were going to be killed."

"I guess so. I don't know. I guess all of this, it's getting to me. I'm sorry."

"There's nothing to be sorry about."

Yes, there was. There was plenty to be sorry about. She wanted Jake, not as a friend, and maybe he even felt the same, at least physically. He desired her. She'd seen that last night, and even now, she could swear that wasn't just her heart she heard pounding. It was his, too.

But he didn't want to take advantage of her. And he'd said that because what had happened between them wasn't anything more than sex to him.

Emotion choked her throat. She reached up, felt something hard against her chest....

Her fingers closed around it. She pulled it away from her, staring down at it in the slash of light that streamed in from the kitchen.

The hair rose on the back of her neck and it took everything inside her to keep from screaming.

"What is this doing on me? I didn't put it on. I

didn't put it on!" She held the silver-and-garnet heart in her fingers.

Lights beaming. Run!

Surreal images flashed through her. She was dreaming, only she was wide awake. The chain felt hot in her cold hands. Burning hot. But at the same time, she was so cold.

She didn't feel herself pushing to her feet. She only knew she was there, standing, staggering backward, clawing at the chain. She heard Jake's voice, as if from a distance.

"Keely—"

"I have to take it off!" She struggled, ripping the necklace over her head.

The heart hit the ground, thudding softly.

Her veins nearly exploded. "Put it back in the box. I don't even want to see it."

Jake reached for it, plucked it up, stuck it in the box on the table. "You don't remember putting it on?"

"No, I don't remember putting it on! I don't want to put it on." She didn't want anything from Ray, especially not this necklace.

She *really* didn't want this necklace.

And she really didn't want to believe there was anything weird about it. She couldn't even put the words together to say what she was thinking. But the words were forming all on their own and she was terrified.

Anything can happen in Haven.... And probably will.

Anything like… A necklace that was *possessed?*

Jake probably already thought she was nuts, the way she was behaving.

"Are you sure you're all right?" His gaze turned on her, worried, intense.

"I'm scared," she whispered. "Jake, what's happening?"

Chapter 13

Keely looked close to a nervous breakdown. And cold. Freezing cold. Her lips were nearly blue and she was shaking.

"I don't know." He hated the helpless feeling inside him. He took his leather jacket, wrapped it around her and pulled her into his arms, held her, and still she shook.

The necklace.

He watched it over Keely's shoulder. "Make it go away," she whispered, her teeth chattering through the words. She turned in his arms, stared back at the piece of jewelry, then back to him. "Put it back in the box."

Stepping around her, he closed the distance to the box, scooping the necklace back inside it in one quick move. He went to the kitchen, grabbed tape out of a drawer, came back and taped the hell out of the box. Keely stood there, looking like she was ready to freak out. He remembered how the box had tumbled toward her out of the rubble. The red lights they'd seen as the quake struck. The voice of Shara Shannon.

Conditions last night, low pressure and dense moisture, combined with an earthquake of that particular magnitude, form the perfect storm.

He'd told Keely he believed anything was possible, but he hadn't taken it that seriously. Now…

"Those red lights—" Keely breathed. She was thinking it, too. She was thinking the same thing he was. "Foundational movement." He saw her throat move. "Foundational movement for paranormal activity, that's what she said. No, that's insane."

Jake didn't know what to tell her. He wrapped his arms around her, held her tightly.

"It's possessed, Jake." She lifted her head, her dark, terror-filled eyes searching his, searching for sanity. "I didn't put it on! It came to me, somehow, in my sleep. Anything can happen in Haven now. Anything. That's what she said."

The mere idea that the necklace held some kind of life of its own was crazy. It shook the very core of everything Jake knew to be true about the natural world.

But this wasn't natural. If what she said was true, this was *supernatural*.

Keely lifted her face to him.

"Tell me you believe me," she whispered. "Tell me I'm not imagining this. Tell me I'm not losing my mind!"

"No." He couldn't believe what was happening, but he knew she needed him to believe her. Could she have put the necklace on in her sleep? All he knew was what she believed and that she needed him to believe her, too. She said she felt strange when she held the necklace, and she was clearly and quite oddly freezing cold. Could she be getting sick? He could find other explanations if he tried…. But he didn't believe them any more than Keely did and that shocked him. Something about that dream of hers seemed too strange when he put it together with the skull she'd found in her garden. "You're not crazy. Or at least if you are, you aren't going crazy alone."

* * *

Her world had been taken over by the unbelievable. From the moment Jake had arrived on her
doorstep and the quake had struck, nothing had
been the same. Ray had been involved in a murder.
And he'd left her this necklace.

And maybe the two of them were connected.

"Sit down," Jake said. "Before you fall down.
Come on. You're freezing. We've got to get you
warmed up."

He'd become her rock in her world gone mad
and she wanted to cling to him when he moved
away, adjusted the thermostat again. She sat on the
couch. He came back, pulled the blanket up around
her. Even with the jacket and the blanket she was
shivering.

"That dream," Jake said. "You woke and found
the necklace on."

She nodded, swallowed hard. "Why me? Why
is the necklace after me?" It lay in the box now,
taped up, still, as if content that they weren't trying
to get rid of it, or leave the house. Not till it got
what it wanted.

What did it want?

"Ray gave the necklace to you," Jake said slowly.
"It's yours now."

"I don't want it!" she cried.

Silence beat heavy. "I don't think you have a choice."

Events beyond her control were taking over her life. Again. She felt anger twine with the relentless fear drumming through her blood.

"What if the necklace is connected to the skull you found?" Jake suggested again. "What if the necklace had been on the body? It belonged to the victim. Somebody killed her—Assuming it was a woman."

The necklace suggested he was correct about the sex of the victim. If there was a victim. If there was even a murder.

"Why would Ray give it to me?"

She wondered if Jake was patronizing her, trying to calm her down by pretending to take her seriously. But the grim light in his eyes belied that thought. He trusted her, and almost as unbelievable as what was happening now, she trusted him.

"Guilt?" he theorized. "He was cheap? It was a convenient gift? Who knows. He got rid of it, wrapped it up like a birthday present. Maybe he didn't even plan on giving it to you, maybe he was just stashing it away and the best way to make sure you didn't poke around in the box if you happened on it was to make it look like a birthday present.

You certainly weren't going to open it right away, you'd wait for your birthday and maybe by then he was going to do something else with it. Who knows. He didn't plan on dying. All we know is that Ray got the necklace, and let's assume he got it off the body. We know there was a body and we know he was digging around in your garden last fall. Tell me about your dream again."

Keely's heart thumped. Was she dreaming. No, not dreaming, *seeing* murder? "I was on a road. It was dark. Lights were coming at me. I knew I was going to be run down. I knew I was going to die."

She knew it like she was there. Like she was seeing it with her own eyes. And she was cold like she was... *Dead.*

Horror burned through her again. She was seeing a murder and she'd woken with that silver-and-garnet heart around her neck.

"Somebody killed her," she gasped. "Somebody ran over her. And they buried her in my garden?" Somebody. Ray. Her heart thumped harder. "The police. We should call the police." The uselessness of that idea hit her immediately. Call the police and tell them what? That her dead husband had left her a demonic necklace? Then they could put her in the crazy bin.

The grim light in Jake's eyes told her he was thinking the same thing. She stared hopelessly at him. "Then what are we going to do?"

"Maybe tomorrow they'll find something more out at your farm," he said. "Maybe those prints they took at your apartment will match up to someone."

"We could be completely offtrack," she said, her mind racing. "Maybe it was just animal bones, like they said. Maybe the break-in at my apartment was random. Maybe—"

"Maybe that necklace didn't jump onto your throat?" Jake held her eyes. "You didn't put it on."

That he believed her was just about the only thing keeping her sanity holding on by a bare thread.

"So what do we do?" she repeated.

He put his hand on hers. "We get through the night." He squeezed her hand, his warmth seeping into her. "We keep you warm."

She swallowed hard. She needed to pull herself together. He put his arms around her, pulling her closer, touching her shoulders, her hair, her face. He was trembling, she realized, as much as she. She wanted him to tell her he could make all this go away.

But he held her and said nothing. He was there for her, that was all he could do for now.

She gazed up at him desperately. "I'm scared of going to sleep again."

He shook his head, his grim eyes shining through the low-lit room. "I won't leave you alone."

Their faces were only inches apart.

This was madness, on some level she knew that. She shouldn't make love to him again. But was it any more mad tonight than it had been last night? She needed him tonight, just as she had before. Only now there was no fooling herself that her heart wouldn't be on the table and that she could get hurt. His gaze was hungry, like hers, and she knew he was thinking the same thing. She was, she realized, his rock in this strange new world, too. With him, she felt warm and alive, not cold and dead.

Then he kissed her and it didn't matter how she would feel later. It only mattered how she felt now.

His fingers ran through her hair, his hands streamed down her back, her body pressed against him. When at last his lips left hers, his eyes gazed into hers, haunted and crackling with a desire that she saw rocked him the way it rocked her. She felt that energy humming between them.

"Make love to me," she whispered, kissing him again. His response was clear from the intensity of his answering kiss. Her shivers fell away, replaced by a deep, hot quivering that shook her just as much.

He pulled back just slightly and the heat of his gaze seared straight through the haunting chill in her bones.

"You'll regret this," he said. "And maybe I will, too, but you will and I can't live with that, Keely."

He was telling her this was just another one-night stand. Okay, two-night stand. He wasn't looking for a permanent relationship, at least not in Haven, maybe not anywhere, anytime.

"I'm not asking for promises," she told him simply. "I'm just asking for tonight."

Rain beat down outside. Wind rattled the small frame of the house. His heartbeat thudded against her own and she knew this was destiny, somehow, some way.

This was wrong, so wrong, but for the life of him Jake couldn't recall why. He'd given up hope since the day he'd watched Brian die. It wasn't just his partner that had blown up in his face. His life had blown up, too. He'd become a machine, a living, breathing machine that couldn't feel, wouldn't let himself feel. Maybe he'd been headed that way for a long time beforehand, too.

And as crazy as the situation was in which he'd found Keely, she was breathing life into him again. Hope and passion and hunger. And he wanted it like he couldn't remember wanting anything before.

She was hurting and scared, but it wasn't just him comforting her—she comforted him, too. He stood there, barely able to breathe, his heart banging so hard against the wall of his chest. He scooped her into his arms, barged through the open door that connected to his bedroom, leaving everything behind—his fears, hers, that damned necklace.

It hit him that the necklace was what had drawn them together, tonight, and maybe last night, too. Was it an accident they'd been trapped in that cellar or part of some supernatural plan he couldn't yet see? Then the thought was lost as he tumbled onto the bed with her and when she reached up to him, there were no more questions. Her hands moved down his back, pulling him closer and she moaned low in her throat as he reached between them to touch his hand to her breast through her shirt.

She pulled back just enough to tear the jacket and shirt off her, baring her taut nipples to his touch. There was no light in the room except for the flashes of lightning coming through the thinly shrouded windows. Greedily, he claimed one tight peak, then another, and she writhed beneath him, those sexy moans driving him wild. Then she was tearing at his clothes, fumbling at his zipper, pushing at his shirt. He helped her rip them off, then she sat up, tugged at her own jeans, leaving nothing but scant panties he could barely see. He dipped his fingers along the sides and pulled them down and off and then she was there, on her back, her skin so smooth and naked and waiting for him.

He possessed her with his hands, his mouth, and she responded with her body arching into him. The smell, the touch, the taste of her wiped everything else away. He claimed her mouth with all the fevered need raging in his soul. Reaching between them, he felt the hot, wet need of her.

Hot, not cold now, as if his heat transferred to her, not just emotionally but physically, warming her to the very core. He felt her release in the way she cried out against his mouth and her body surged against his hand, then she reached for him, desperate, shaking, guiding him inside her.

Take it slow, he told himself. God, he wanted this to be slow. He wanted this to last forever.

The shock of that thought jammed hard into his chest, then she rocked into him, sweeping him away in the gut-wrenching sweetness of her cries.

He swallowed them with his mouth, plunging deeper inside her, as deep as he could go. They rocked together and he came hard and fast and they lay panting, clinging together as if for survival

"I can't get enough of you, Keely," he breathed raspily against her ear. She pulled over top of him, straddling him, clinging to him still, clinging to his heat, and he couldn't believe how quickly he was ready for her again. She sheathed him inside her, ready, too, and he thrust upward, softer, gentler, longer, the rhythmic pattern taking them higher, every breath a whimper, a low moan of perfect pleasure, until they climbed the stars together.

She collapsed, damp and sweet and warm, in the crook of his shoulder. He wrapped his arms around her and held her close. Nothing was going to happen to her tonight.

Light laced through the thin curtains barely veiling the morning fingers of dawn. She was… In Jake's house. In Jake's bed.

In Jake's arms.

Turning her head, she saw him beside her, sleeping soundly. He looked wonderful naked, all powerful shoulders and bare, sculpted chest tapering to a lean waist, and lower…. Remembered desire drummed through her. He stole her senses and probably he'd steal her peace of mind for a good, long time to come. And yet she felt some odd peace anyway. He'd shown her that she could live again. She didn't have to hold herself alone forever just because Ray hadn't been the man she'd needed.

And if she needed Jake and he didn't choose to be that man… She would survive. She felt the first pang of heartbreak. She'd thought one night was enough, but now she knew two was not enough, either.

Their clothes were scattered on the floor. His handgun lay on the nightstand beside him, ready. He was ready to protect her, ready for anything.

She shut her eyes suddenly against the flash of renewed fear, the puzzlelike pieces of the night before ramming into her then scattering in a kaleidoscope of colors, unsolved. The skull, the strange white truck bursting out of her barn, the break-in at her apartment, the necklace…

None of it made sense. Ray had left her this nightmare. But at least Jake was by her side to solve it.

They *had* to solve it. The possessed necklace was possessing her. They could hardly take a nightmare and a crazy tale of a supernatural piece of jewelry to the police. The necklace belonged to her now, had been given to her. The necklace wanted her to find the truth. Justice, maybe?

The chill from last night crept into her again as she sat up in the bed. The heaviness around her neck seeped into her consciousness. Something hard and cold, a cold that she felt even now seeping down deep inside her, hung between her breasts. She reached up her hand, grasped the silver-and-garnet heart and gasped. It was hanging around her neck. Hanging. The chain had repaired itself. And the necklace had come to her again.

Jake opened his eyes as she swung her gaze to his, and held it for a horror-stretched beat.

"It's back," she whispered.

Chapter 14

The stark, haunted light of her eyes tore Jake's heart out. She held herself very still, as if afraid to move. But she was moving, involuntarily. She was starting to shiver. Last night, he'd warmed her up. But this morning, the necklace was back and it was freezing her again.

"I'm going to take it off you," he said slowly, steadily, knowing she was so scared right now, any sudden move could frighten her more. He wanted to protect her, and he didn't know how because he didn't know what he was protecting her from.

He reached for the chain and she turned her head, pulling at the thick gold-spun hair to move it out of his way. The nape of her neck was ice to his touch. He unclasped the necklace, reaching around to let it fall into his palm.

Her skin was smooth and pale, naked. The bedsheet twisted at her waist, her breasts falling heavy and beautiful against her chest.

"You're cold," he said. "Take the blanket." He shrugged the sheet from him along with the blanket, tucking it all around her. She scrunched eagerly into it, still shivering.

He stared down at the necklace in his hand. He hadn't examined it closely the night before. The silver was slightly tarnished, as she'd mentioned, as if it had been cleaned, perhaps by Ray, but not with attention to detail. There were five little garnets encrusted into the silver. They were small, not worth much, he guessed, though he was no connoisseur of jewels. It looked harmless in the dawn sun, but it held secrets. What did the necklace want from them, from Keely?

Turning the heart over, he saw the initials I.L.K.

"What is it?" Keely asked.

He shifted the back of the heart toward her so that she could see it in the light. "Initials. I.L.K."

He raised his gaze to her. "Know anyone with those initials?"

She shook her head.

He ran his fingers over the heart, looking for a clue, anything that would tell them more—

A thin ridge rode all along the sides, clear around the heart. His finger stopped on a tiny indentation.

"It's a locket," he said suddenly.

"What?"

"It's a locket." His pulse pounded. The heart was so slim, so flat, that hadn't occurred to him. He dipped the edge of his nail, pressed hard against the indentation, and the heart sprang open.

The picture inside was faded, but the faces were visible. The sides were black, making him think of those photo booths at carnivals where you paid five bucks and got a series of pictures in strips. The faces were smiling at the camera, heads together. Teenagers. A girl and a boy, maybe seventeen or eighteen. A sense of giddiness pervaded the photo. The girl was dark-haired, doe-eyed, her eyes turned toward the boy at her side. The boy gazed straight-on at the camera, through glasses, and despite the years that had to have passed between then and now, Jake recognized him. He'd met him last night.

"That's Tom," Keely breathed.

Tom Tanner, town manager of Haven, husband of one of Keely's closest friends…

"Tom and who?" Jake asked.

"I don't know." He could see her swallow hard, see her confusion. "Tom dated Lise all through high school, then all through college. Except for a few weeks when they broke up and Lise went out with Jud Peterson. That was their senior year, I think. I was a few years behind them. They ran around together and I wasn't so much a part of their crowd then. I knew Lise more from church. Her family was friends with my family. I used to get her hand-me-downs…." She put shaking fingers to her mouth. "What does this mean? Tom dated whoever this girl is, and this is the girl who was killed, the girl whose skull I found in my garden?"

"Maybe." Jake worked to process what they knew so far. "Assuming this is the girl who owned the necklace—and I think that's pretty safe—then we guess that's her body that was buried in your garden. If your visions are real, then she was killed, run down on the road. Maybe it was even an accident. Maybe Ray helped him take care of it, hide the body. Then they moved it last fall…."

Jake dropped the necklace on the bed, got up to

grab fresh jeans and a shirt from the bag he hadn't even unpacked yet.

"I did some checking on the Internet last night, while you were sleeping," he went on, zipping his pants as he continued. He was speculating, maybe still wildly, but they were getting closer to something, maybe the truth. "Tom Tanner pushed the town hard to buy some land last fall. The town lost out to a developer."

"The new Maple Creek subdivision," Keely said. Her eyes followed him as he paced the room. She didn't touch the necklace, as if she still feared it and the secrets it held, secrets it seemed to want to convey.

"Maybe they'd buried the body out there. Maybe that's why they moved it. Maybe Ray took care of the job."

"Why would Ray do it if Tom was the one who—" Suggesting Tom was a killer seemed no less easy for Keely than that it could have been her late husband.

Tom was still alive and Tom was married to her friend. An old friend. A friend whose somewhat perfect life might be about to shatter.

"Ray must have known about it. Somehow. Maybe he was in the car with Tom that night, or maybe Tom went to him for help. Was he part of the crowd that Tom ran around with?"

"Yes. Tom and Ray, sometimes Jud, till Tom and Lise broke up and Lise went out with Jud for awhile. She and Tom got back together around the time I started seeing Ray. That's when I started getting closer with Lise."

Jake remembered how upset Lise had been last night with Tom for giving money to Jud. He used to do a drunken half-ass job for money, but now Jud wanted nothing but handouts.

"Jud found out about the murder. Maybe he was blackmailing Tom," he suggested. "Maybe Ray was, too. You said he had money to buy things at estate sales to stock at the store but you had no idea where the money came from. And Jud and Ray had been friends. Maybe he clued Jud in about the body. Maybe he even helped Ray move it."

Blood money. Maybe Ray had had blood money.

Keely paled. "But if Tom knew about the locket—"

"He knew Ray had given you a gift. Everyone at the party last night knew Ray had given you a gift. Then someone broke in to your apartment."

"Tom and Lise were still at the party when we left," Keely pointed out.

."Tom talked to Jud on the phone."

"That was before the gift from Ray was brought up."

"Lise brought it up. She could have mentioned it to Tom earlier."

"You just said maybe Jud was blackmailing him," Keely argued. "Now you think he asked Jud to break into my apartment?"

"He was already paying him. Maybe he wanted more for his money."

"But if Tom knew this girl, whoever she was, had this locket on her when she died, a locket with a picture of him with her, why would he have buried her with the locket in the first place?"

"Maybe he didn't realize she had it on her. It was nighttime, dark, in your dream, right?"

Keely nodded.

"Maybe he had no idea at the time. He was in a hurry—and in a panic. Maybe he called on Ray to help him cover it up, help him get rid of the body. That would be manslaughter and a boy like Tom with college plans ahead of him would see those dreams being ruined if he didn't cover it up. But he knew where the body was and he didn't want it going to a developer—and when it did, he arranged to have the body moved, called on his old friend again.

"And this time maybe," he went on, "it wasn't dark and maybe Ray found the locket and decided the body hadn't been safe once and if it ever wasn't safe again, he was going to make sure he had some evidence linking it back to Tom, evidence he could use for his own purposes, blackmail. He wrapped it up, hid it in the house like a birthday present, probably planned to do something else with it later but then he died...."

Keely drew a shaky breath. "You have a lot of maybe's there."

"Yeah," he said grimly. A lot of maybe's. "But the biggest maybe is that maybe it's all true."

Keely rubbed her palm over the steamy mirror in the apartment bathroom. She'd opened the store and called Tammy to come in early. Picking up her comb, she drew it through the tangles in her hair. Depression weighed her down and she was annoyed with herself.

She'd gone into that bedroom with Jake last night with her eyes wide open. He wasn't looking for a relationship, and truth was, neither was she. That she was falling in more than lust with Jake was a side issue she'd deal with on her own. He cared about her, obviously, but that wasn't enough.

She'd had a relationship that was less than enough before. He'd made her want a relationship again. Shocking. But she wasn't settling. She couldn't settle. She couldn't put herself through that kind of hell again.

She wanted his love and he'd made it plain he didn't even believe in the concept.

He was waiting for her outside the bathroom when she finished dressing. He lifted those dark, smoldering eyes to her that made her feel hot inside even when she was still cold. She'd dressed warmly despite the spring day. A pervasive chill carried clear to her bones.

"You can't be my bodyguard," she said. "I don't want one and I don't need one."

The apartment phone, the same line that connected with the store office downstairs, rang. Keely picked it up.

"This is Trooper Nielson. Keely Schiffer?"

Keely's pulse thudded automatically. Trooper Nielson was the officer who'd handled the break-in call the night before. "Yes?"

"The prints came up quickly," he said. "We had them right here in our office, didn't even have to put them through the state's. They belonged to Jud Peterson."

Keely's stomach dipped. "Jud Peterson? He's the one who broke into my apartment last night?"

If it had been Jud last night, then that was one maybe of Jake's that was true and what did that mean about the rest of his maybe's?

"We went out to his home this morning," the trooper continued. "We found Jud Peterson dead. Gunshot wound to the head. He also had a white pickup truck, with front side dents. We're checking tire patterns to see if that was the vehicle that Jake Malloy reported trying to run him down out at your farm."

Keely gasped. "Oh, my God." She lifted a shaking hand to her lips, moved the phone to whisper to Jake, "Jud's dead. Someone shot him. He had a white truck!" And where would Jud get the money for a truck? He certainly didn't earn it….

"Let me talk to the officer."

Keely stood by while Jake asked a few more questions, experiencing a mix of comfort and anxiety as he morphed into grim cop mode.

"We have reason to believe the victim out at the farm could have had the initials I.L.K. and that Tom Tanner was involved," Jake was saying. He told them about the possible connection to the property sold to the developer last fall. "Bring in Tom Tanner for questioning."

They'd had nothing but an unbelievable paranormal experience and conjecture before. Now the police had a new murder. Now they'd pay attention.

"What'd they say?" she asked when he hung up.

"They found some bones out at your farm this morning," he told her.

"What do we do? Do they believe us? Are they going to talk to Tom?"

"Now that they have two bodies on their hands, a new one and an old one, they're taking what we have to say more seriously. They're going to pick up Tom and I'm going to take the necklace to the station. They want it to take in to evidence now. They're going to show it to Tom, see what they can shake out of him."

"He might not talk. Or we might even be wrong."

"Either way, whoever did it will find out you don't have the necklace anymore. You'll be safe, out of it. If Tom was responsible for the death of I.L.K., it's going to be difficult to prove after all this time. But if he was responsible for Jud Peterson's death, that's a different story and the necklace, coming from Ray and the bones being found in your garden, could tie the two crimes together."

"He took a big chance, if he killed Jud."

"If he's the one who killed I.L.K., then he's got a lot to lose," Jake pointed out. "Then and now. What's one more murder? In for a penny, in for a pound. He knows there's still a chance he'll get away with it. He has no choice but to take the chance if he knows this locket could connect him to those bones. Now we know the necklace was what they were after from you. I'll give it to the police, and you make sure everyone in this town knows you don't have it anymore. Ray didn't leave you anything else, did he?"

Keely laughed harshly. "Debts."

The silence in the room felt heavy.

The phone rang.

Keely picked it up.

"Hey. Do you need me to come into the store today?"

She put her hand over the phone. "It's Lise," she whispered. Hurt waved through her. If Tom had done everything they thought he had, Lise's life was going to be shattered terribly.

"Tell her to come in," Jake said. "In case Tom goes nuts, it'll get her out of harm's way."

Keely asked Lise to come in at ten then hung

up. "I hope she's okay. Oh, God, what I hope is that it wasn't Tom, after all."

Jake nodded. "I hope so, too."

He left for the station with the necklace, still in the box, and Keely was unbelievably relieved to see it go. Whatever had happened with that necklace last night, she wanted it to be over. She wanted that necklace out of her life.

The store remained busy, though not quite as bad as the day before. She made a big point of telling people she'd turned a necklace Ray left her over to the police. She plowed her way through the morning, feeling warmer as the day progressed. Thank God. The necklace was gone and so was its strange power over her. The more hours passed, the less she could even believe what had happened, with the necklace and with Jake.

When they needed extra hands at the short-order counter, she went to the kitchen, happy to be busy.

She took a full bag of trash out back to the Dumpster. It was nearly noon and the birds were singing and the air felt good. She was still alive, and as long as she was alive, she had hope. Jake had at least shown her that she could live again, even love again.

Back inside, she found Mary waiting outside her office.

"Hey, brat," Mary said. "What's up?"

Keely had a hard time suddenly controlling the tears. The happiness fell away as reality hit her. It'd been hard keeping things to herself all day with Lise at the store, knowing how her life could be about to shatter. She needed to confide in someone.

"Let's go in my office," she said.

Mary came in, shutting the door behind her. "What's wrong?"

Keely refrained from teasing her friend that she should already know, seeing as how she was psychic. Then Mary surprised her.

"I know something's wrong," she said gravely. "There's something about that skull back at your farm."

"They found more bones today. It's real." Keely shivered.

"That necklace… It was a locket, wasn't it? I keep seeing a man and a woman, and there's some kind of danger, Keely. Danger to you!"

Keely swallowed hard. "I'm scared," she admitted. "The police have the necklace now." She told Mary about waking with the locket around her neck, about the vision. If there was anyone who would believe her in this town, it was Mary. She was afraid to say anything about Tom Tanner. There was always Danny…. He'd run around with that crowd, too. She didn't want to scare Mary.

Mary already looked scared. "I think there's more. What aren't you telling me?"

Maybe she really was psychic now. Anything was believable.

"I'm seeing something," Mary said suddenly. Her eyes widened. "There's something, papers, that's it. Papers. Papers from Ray. Do you have any papers from Ray?"

"Papers? No, just, well, his manuscripts. But that was fiction."

"Are you sure? Where are they?"

"He kept them in a bank deposit box." She'd always thought that was strange. Fear raced straight to her bones. What if it was more than strange? He'd never seemed to do anything with his writing. What if it hadn't all been fiction? What if he'd written down what happened in case anything ever happened to him? She'd completely forgotten about them.

Ray didn't leave you anything else, did he?

Chapter 15

"Oh, my God," Keely breathed. "I have to go get those papers."

"I'm going with you," Mary said.

The bank was within walking distance. She told Tammy where they were going and once inside the bank, she explained that she didn't have the key. She had no idea what Ray had done with it, but she didn't have it and if it was in the house, she'd never find it now. Thank God for small towns and people who'd known her since birth and broke the rules.

The box contained one slim legal-size envelope, not the piles of manuscripts she might have expected.

Mary was waiting for her when she came out of the vault. "Let's go back and get your car," Keely said. "I want to take this to the police station. I'll open it there."

Mary nodded. "Okay. Good idea."

They got back to the store parking lot and found Lise by her car. She turned and Keely saw the tears in her eyes.

"Tom's at the police station," Lise choked out. "I have to get there." She started sobbing.

Oh, God she was in no shape to drive. And she knew. She knew about Tom. The news wasn't going to get any better, either. Keely put her arms around her friend, looking at Mary over Lise's shoulder. "Come on. Come with us."

Lise got in the back. It was only a mile up the road to the police station. Keely looked back at Lise after they pulled out of the parking lot. "Are you o—"

She wasn't crying anymore. "Just drive," Lise said, the small pistol she'd pulled out of somewhere suddenly jammed against the back of Mary's head. "And keep driving."

* * *

It took four hours for Tom Tanner to crack under police examination while Jake, by professional courtesy, was allowed to watch and listen behind a concealed observation window, and when he finally did crack Jake knew he'd made the biggest mistake of his life. And once again, someone was going to die.

Someone he felt more than protectiveness toward, and the fear he'd felt about that was completely gone in the face of danger. He was going to lose her.

"I really hate to do this to you guys."

She had a gun. Lise had a gun. Her friend Lise had a gun and she was pointing it at the back of Mary's head while she continued to drive. The car swung wide, nearly running into a guardrail as they wildly rounded a sharp curve.

Keely's heart pounded. "Then maybe you shouldn't do this," she said. *What was Lise going to do?*

"No, I'm going to do it. I just feel bad about it, I want you to know that."

Lise sounded shockingly calm. Like this was no big deal. And she didn't really sound like she felt bad about it.

"Why?" Her mouth felt thick. Fear. Fear was taking over her. She was almost afraid she'd pass out from it, but she had to keep her wits about her. She had to do something. What? They were careening down the highway out of Haven at fifty miles an hour down a winding, sharply curving road through mountain hollows. They whipped by a two-story farmhouse. A horse munched grass behind a wooden post fence in a field beside it. A trembling Mary just barely missed hitting the mailbox by the road. The serene country scenery contrasted sickly with the nightmare playing out inside the car.

"You know why, you idiot," Lise said. "You found that damn locket. If we hadn't been in such a drunken mess that night, we'd have realized she was wearing it."

"We? Who's we?" Who all was involved? Keely's head reeled.

"Me and Tom and Ray and Jud. We were drunk, driving around, too many of us piled in a car with too much alcohol. Stupid! And then Tom tells us that moron Ilene Klasko was pregnant—he was going to leave me even though we'd just gotten back together."

Ilene Klasko. I.L.K. Keely didn't know an Ilene

Klasko, but she had to have been a couple classes ahead of her in school, like Danny and Tom and Ray and Jud. Mary had been in Keely's class, but Mary had started dating Danny long before Keely'd hooked up with Ray—

"I swear to God, it was an accident," Lise said, angry now, the hand holding the gun shaking. Shaking but still pointing at Mary. "I wanted to go see her. I told Tom to tell her to get an abortion. We went to her house and he told her, then we backed out, turned back around and Ilene was standing in the damn road. It was so dark, we didn't see her till the last minute. She was running and I was trying to brake. I was trying! I was drunk. And I was angry, dammit. I hit her and—"

She broke off.

Lise had hit her. Lise had been driving.

"It was all Tom's fault," Lise snarled. "He should have gotten that property for the town. Then it would have been a nature preserve and we wouldn't have had to do a thing. Everything got screwed up then. We buried her there, all of us. We were scared, okay? Scared!"

Her eyes burned. "We wrote letters to her mom, said she'd run away, signed them from Ilene. Tom had some notes from her, so we faked her handwriting. Her mom's a drug addict, and she was in jail the next year. Ilene's older sister ran away the year before. Nobody ever expected Ilene to do any different. Nobody cared! Ilene disappeared and *nobody cared*. Her mom didn't even make a police report. It was perfect."

Perfectly horrible. Keely's mind spun. All this time, her friends had been involved in this awful secret. Ray, too.

Then Ray had up and died in an accident, leaving that locket and his manuscript. She hadn't even looked at it yet, but she knew what it had to be. Mary knew, somehow.

"What's in those papers of Ray's?" Keely asked, wanting to hear Lise say it.

"He said if anything ever happened to him, if any of us ever did anything to hurt him— He said he'd left something behind that would be found after his death. He said he'd written it all down. We weren't that worried about it. We knew you'd think it was his damn fiction. Then you found the skull. Then everything changed."

They knew she wouldn't think it was fiction now. Her throat all but closed up in horror. It could have stayed secret forever if she hadn't found Ilene's skull. And if the locket hadn't revealed too much truth…

Jake was with the police. He was with Tom. Maybe Lise didn't think Tom would break, but maybe he would.

But even if he did, it could be too late for her.

"That developer bought that old farm," Lise was saying. "So Ray said he'd move the body. He wouldn't tell anybody what he'd done with it, but he started talking about the locket, getting money out of Tom. Then Jud wanted money, too. Tom was the only one who had any, at least that kind of money. He sent Jud to your apartment last night but he screwed up again and he was going to go to the cops when Tom threatened him. Tom killed him. He didn't tell me he did, but I know he did. It's the second time Jud screwed up—he was supposed to dig up the rest of the bones but he didn't get them all. He got scared when that damn Jake Malloy came out there and nearly ran him down trying to get away. Jud was a liability. I had to fix it. I have to fix everything."

Keely knew she was a liability now, too. Now that Lise had Ray's papers, Keely was expendable.

"Tom's at the police station," she said sharply. "You aren't going to get away with this, Lise. If you hurt us, you aren't going to get away with it. They'll show Tom the picture in the locket. They know he was involved with Ilene somehow. And they found those bones at my farm. They'll start putting it together, and there'll be some evidence, some kind of DNA, that'll connect up to Jud's murder. It's all falling apart. Don't make it worse!"

She wanted to beg, but she didn't think that would work. She had to try reason.

And she had to get out of this car. Wherever Lise was taking them, nothing good could happen there. They'd make her and Mary disappear, just like they'd made Ilene Klasko disappear. And Lise was crazy.

"They're going to find out, Lise. Tom's going to tell them everything!"

"They're not going to know. Tom isn't going to break and tell them. He knows I was going to figure out some way to get Ray's papers. Nobody's going to tell. I'm going to fix it."

They'd been covering up this crime for so long, Lise couldn't believe it would all come apart. And she was going to kill them. Hopelessness swamped Keely. A car came toward them from the other direction. She needed help, but she had no idea how to get it.

"I'm sorry, I really am, but I'll get over it," Lise said with a hard laugh. "I'll even feel bad about it for a little— Oh, my God!"

Keely jerked her head to the front windshield of the car, following Mary's suddenly horrified gaze. She couldn't see anything, just winding blacktop and the other car, but she felt a biting wave of cold rushing over her bones.

"Get out of the road," Lise screamed. "Oh, my God! Ilene!"

The car spun out of control. All Keely knew then was the rush of trees coming at her, too fast, too blinding.

She had no idea how much time passed before she woke. She felt heat, terrible heat. Opening her eyes painfully, she saw Mary, head thrown on the steering wheel, completely still. Lise, too, was still—thrown clear out of the front window.

Something hissed.

The engine was going to catch on fire. The engine. Keely's head reeled with pain and she felt herself passing out. She couldn't keep her eyes open. Arms reached for her. The door of the car was open, somehow. Arms reached for her, pulled her to safety, depositing her gently on the sloping pine-covered bank. They were over the river. She could hear the sound of water swishing through rocks over the hissing of the car. Only a line of trees had stopped them from careening into the water.

She opened her eyes. A girl she recognized smiled down at her. Keely blinked, hard, her vision wavering. She reached up, tried to touch the girl, but her hand went... Right through her.

Ilene Klasko. The name burst through her head. "Ilene?" she whispered brokenly.

The girl smiled and the vision of her fell apart, disintegrating. She sensed Mary laying down next to her. And then all she could see was smoke and flames and all she could hear was the sound of sirens. The other car... Someone had seen the accident. Someone had called for help.

She struggled to sit up, still afraid. The car was going to explode. She crawled, desperate.

Then something grabbed at her ankle and she felt the business end of a gun at the back of her head.

Jake scrambled down the embankment, past trees, sliding, down to the bottom where smoke choked the air and seared his lungs. "Keely!"

He hadn't waited for the officers coming behind him when the call had come in reporting an accident. The car they'd described fit with Mary's. Mary had gone to get Keely and Ray's papers, they knew that from calling the store to look for Keely. Tom had spilled everything. Lise had run down

Ilene Klasko years ago, and he had killed Jud after he'd failed to fix things at the farmhouse yesterday morning. They'd all participated in covering up the old crime. Tom had transformed from a coolly elegant, almost academic, politician to a quivering, weeping mess. Jake had no sympathy for him.

He could only pray he wasn't too late for Keely and Mary, the innocents in this complicated, dark drama. The sirens came closer and he stopped short feet beside the car, searching inside.

There was no one there.

He swung around, backing away. The car could explode and only the fear that Keely was inside had brought him that close.

"Jake!"

He pivoted, saw them through the trees, Lise shoving Keely ahead of her. He could see Mary now, on the ground near them, not moving. Lise grabbed Keely by the hair when she didn't get up fast enough, swung her arm around and he saw the gun pointed straight at him.

Keely rose up suddenly, shoved Lise forward. The other woman lost her footing, dropping the gun. Keely was on it in two seconds, tackling Lise, putting that same gun to the back of her friend's neck. Her shocked gaze jerked to Jake's.

"Jake!" Keely screamed.

It was too late when he realized why she was screaming. Keely was okay, but he wasn't.

The force of the vehicle's explosion knocked him to the ground even as he saw Keely throwing herself down atop Mary and covering her own head from the blast. He heard officers shouting. As he fought off blackness, he knew Keely was okay.

"Jake," he heard her crying. It was Keely, he knew it was Keely. He heard shouts, officers barking orders. They were taking Lise into custody and getting medics for Mary.

But Keely, she was here, by his side, despite the flaming heat still too near.

He couldn't get up. God, he wanted to get up. He had to work to lift his eyelids, focus hard to make even one bit of his body obey his directions.

Her sexy, drop-dead, drown-in-me eyes seared his gaze.

"Don't die on me now," she whispered. "Don't you dare die on me now. I need you," she went on sweetly. God, he loved her voice. "I need you." She wasn't in danger anymore, but she still needed him….

"I'm not going to die," he promised. "But I

think I'm going to black out." He grabbed her arm, focusing desperately on her, keeping himself conscious by sheer force of his will. He felt himself floating. "I just have to know one thing."

"Anything."

"I'm thinking about falling in love with you." Maybe he was in love with her already. And it felt right. Real. Perspective. He was about to pass out and he'd finally found perspective. "Is that okay?"

He heard the sob Keely caught in her throat. "I thought you didn't believe in love."

A laugh rose inside him but it hurt too much. He hurt everywhere. He'd hit the ground hard. And he was losing it fast. He had to tell her. She had to believe, the way she'd made him believe.

"You're not going to start arguing now, are you?" he said. "I want you to believe me."

"I do," she choked out, "I believe you."

"Anything can happen in Haven," he whispered roughly. "Anything."

Her tears were falling fast. He felt first one then another hit his face as she leaned down to kiss him. "And probably will," she cried. "And probably will."

Epilogue

Recovery came in little bits, a day at a time, for Keely, for Jake, for the whole town. She'd lost a lot…her house, Tom and Lise. Ray's writings had been a fictional account of the night Ilene Lauren Klasko had been run down, in a drunken accident by a car full of teenagers who'd panicked and covered it up.

The manuscript hadn't been finished. The ending was still working its way through the courts.

But for all Keely had lost, most days she woke

thinking of what she'd gained. A new sense of her self, a new courage and confidence. And Jake.

They'd level-jumped on their relationship, as he'd said once. They took things slow now. They dated. He quit his job on the force in Charleston and picked up with the Haven P.D. The small force needed his big-city experience and was glad to have him.

Sometimes they talked about marriage and the future, but mostly they talked about today. What they didn't talk about much was the necklace, though she'd told Jake about the girl, the ghost of Ilene, and how she'd saved her. She'd known Jake would believe her. Mary believed her, of course. Mary had seen Ilene, too, and was struggling now with her own demons as she recovered from the ordeal. She'd stopped doing psychic readings. It all had become too real for Mary. Keely wasn't so sure about the rest of the town, though she heard rumors of other people having strange experiences. Whispers. Gossip at the store. Some people believed what Shara Shannon had said about the quake. Some people didn't. Some people, like Keely, kept it to themselves. Looking back, it seemed impossible, too impossible to be real.

Her life had been changed by that necklace. It

had brought her truth, and it had brought her Jake. Whatever had happened, if she'd just been a little sick with chills and if she'd put that necklace on in her sleep... If that vision had just been a coincidental dream... And if she and Mary had gotten out of that about-to-explode car on their own...

It didn't matter. Somehow, it had all brought her life together with Jake's. She knew what she believed and it didn't matter what anyone else thought about it.

Anything could happen in Haven. Even love.

Award-winning author Stevi Mittman delivers
another hysterical mystery, featuring Teddi
Bayer, an irrepressible heroine, and her to-
die-for hero, Detective Drew Scoones. After
all, life on Long Island can be murder!

*Turn the page for a sneak peek at the warm and
funny fourth book,
WHOSE NUMBER IS UP, ANYWAY?
in the Teddi Bayer series,
by STEVI MITTMAN.
On sale August 7*

CHAPTER 1

"Before redecorating a room, I always advise
my clients to empty it of everything but one
chair. Then I suggest they move that chair
from place to place, sitting in it, until the
placement feels right. Trust your instincts
when deciding on furniture placement. Your
room should 'feel right.'"

—TipsFromTeddi.com

Gut feelings. You know, that gnawing in the pit
of your stomach that warns you that you are about
to do the absolute stupidest thing you could do?
Something that will ruin life as you know it?

I've got one now, standing at the butcher counter in King Kullen, the grocery store in the same strip mall as L.I. Lanes, the bowling alley cum billiard parlor I'm in the process of redecorating for its "Grand Opening."

I realize being in the wrong supermarket probably doesn't sound exactly dire to you, but you aren't the one buying your father a brisket at a store your mother will somehow know isn't Waldbaum's.

And then, June Bayer isn't your mother.

The woman behind the counter has agreed to go into the freezer to find a brisket for me, since there aren't any in the case. There are packages of pork tenderloin, piles of spare ribs and rolls of sausage, but no briskets.

Warning Number Two, right? I should be so out of here.

But no, I'm still in the same spot when she comes back out, brisketless, her face ashen. She opens her mouth as if she is going to scream, but only a gurgle comes out.

And then she pinballs out from behind the counter, knocking bottles of Peter Luger Steak Sauce to the floor on her way, now hitting the tower of cans at the end of the prepared foods aisle and sending them sprawling, now making her way down the aisle, careening from side to side as she goes.

Finally, from a distance, I hear her shout, "He's deeeeeeaaaad! Joey's deeeeeaaaad."

My first thought is *You should always trust your gut.*

My second thought is that now, somehow, my mother will know I was in King Kullen. For weeks I will have to hear "What did you expect?" as though whenever you go to King Kullen someone turns up dead. And if the detective investigating the case turns out to be Detective Drew Scoones…well, I'll never hear the end of that from her, either.

She still suspects I murdered the guy who was found dead on my doorstep last Halloween just to get Drew back into my life.

Several people head for the butcher's freezer and I position myself to block them. If there's one thing I've learned from finding people dead—and the guy on my doorstep wasn't the first one—it's that the police get very testy when you mess with their murder scenes.

"You can't go in there until the police get here," I say, stationing myself at the end of the butcher's counter and in front of the Employees Only door,

acting as if I'm some sort of authority. "You'll con-
taminate the evidence if it turns out to be murder."

Shouts and chaos. You'd think I'd know better
than to throw the word *murder* around. Cell phones
are flipping open and tongues are wagging.

I amend my statement quickly. "Which, of
course, it probably isn't. Murder, I mean. People
die all the time, and it's not always in hospitals or
their own beds, or…" I babble when I'm nervous,
and the idea of someone dead on the other side of
the freezer door makes me very nervous.

So does the idea of seeing Drew Scoones again.
Drew and I have this on-again, off-again sort of
thing…that I kind of turned off.

Who knew he'd take it so personally when he
tried to get serious and I responded by saying we
could talk about *us* tomorrow—and then caught a
plane to my parents' condo in Boca the next day?
In July. In the middle of a job.

For some crazy reason, he took that to mean that
I was avoiding him and the subject of *us*.

That was three months ago. I haven't seen him
since.

The manager, who identifies himself and points
to his nameplate in case I don't believe him, says
he has to go into *his cooler*. "Maybe Joey's not

dead," he says. "Maybe he can be saved, and you're letting him die in there. Did you ever think of that?"

In fact, I hadn't. But I had thought that the murderer might try to go back in to make sure his tracks were covered, so I say that I will go in and check.

Which means that the manager and I couple up and go in together while everyone pushes against the doorway to peer in, erasing any chance of finding clean prints on that Employee Only door.

I expect to find carcasses of dead animals hanging from hooks, and maybe Joey hanging from one, too. I think it's going to be very creepy and I steel myself, only to find a rather benign series of shelves with large slabs of meat laid out carefully on them, along with boxes and boxes marked simply Chicken.

Nothing scary here, unless you count the body of a middle-aged man with graying hair sprawled faceup on the floor. His eyes are wide open and un-blinking. His shirt is stiff. His pants are stiff. His body is stiff. And his expression, you should forgive the pun—is frozen. Bill-the-manager crosses himself and stands mute while I pronounce the guy dead in a sort of *happy now?* tone.

"We should not be in here," I say, and he nods his head emphatically and helps me push people out of the doorway just in time to hear the police sirens and see the cop cars pull up outside the big store windows.

Bobbie Lyons, my partner in Teddi Bayer Interior Designs (and also my neighbor, my best friend and my private fashion police), and Mark, our carpenter (and my dogsitter, confidant, and ego booster), rush in from next door. They beat the cops by a half step and shout out my name. People point in my direction.

After all the publicity that followed the unfortunate incident during which I shot my ex-husband, Rio Gallo, and then the subsequent murder of my first client—which I solved, I might add—it seems like the whole world, or at least all of Long Island, knows who I am.

Mark asks if I'm all right. (Did I remember to mention that the man is drop-dead-gorgeous-but-a-decade-too-young-for-me-yet-too-old-for-my-daughter-thank-god?) I don't get a chance to answer him because the police are quickly closing in on the store manager and me.

"The woman—" I begin telling the police. Then I have to pause for the manager to fill in her name, which he does: *Fran.*

I continue. "Right. Fran. Fran went into the

freezer to get a brisket. A moment later she came out and screamed that Joey was dead. So I'd say she was the one who discovered the body."

"And you are…?" the cop asks me. It comes out a bit like who do I *think* I am, rather than who am I really?

"An innocent bystander," Bobbie, hair perfect, makeup just right, says, carefully placing her body between the cop and me.

"And she was just leaving," Mark adds. They each take one of my arms.

Fran comes into the inner circle surrounding the cops. In case it isn't obvious from the hairnet and bloodstained white apron with Fran embroidered on it, I explain that she was the butcher who was going for the brisket. Mark and Bobbie take that as a signal that I've done my job and they can now get me out of there. They twist around, with me in the middle, as if we're a Rockettes line, until we are facing away from the butcher counter. They've managed to propel me a few steps toward the exit when disaster—in the form of a Mazda RX7 pulling up at the loading curb—strikes.

Mark's grip on my arm tightens like a vise. "Too late," he says.

Bobbie's expletive is unprintable. "Maybe

there's a back door," she suggests, but Mark is right. It's too late.

I've laid my eyes on Detective Scoones. And while my gut is trying to warn me that my heart shouldn't go there, regions farther south are melting at just the sight of him.

"Walk," Bobbie orders me.

And I try to. Really.

Walk, I tell my feet. *Just put one foot in front of the other.*

I can do this because I know, in my heart of hearts, that if Drew Scoones was still interested in me, he'd have gotten in touch with me after I returned from Boca. And he didn't.

Since he's a detective, Drew doesn't have to wear one of those dark blue Nassau County Police uniforms. Instead, he's got on jeans, a tight-fitting T-shirt and a tweedy sports jacket. If you think that sounds good, you should see him. Chiseled features, cleft chin, brown hair that's naturally a little sandy in the front, a smile that…well, that doesn't matter. He isn't smiling now.

He walks up to me, tucks his sunglasses into his breast pocket and looks me over from head to toe.

"Well, if it isn't Miss Cut and Run," he says. "Aren't you supposed to be somewhere in Florida or something?" He looks at Mark accusingly, as if he was covering for me when he told Drew I was gone.

"Detective Scoones?" one of the uniforms says. "The stiff's in the cooler and the woman who found him is over there." He jerks his head in Fran's direction.

Drew continues to stare at me.

You know how when you were young, your mother always told you to wear clean underwear in case you were in an accident? And how, a little farther on, she told you not to go out in hair rollers because you never knew who you might see—or who might see you? And how now your best friend says she wouldn't be caught dead without makeup and suggests you shouldn't either?

Okay, today, *finally,* in my overalls and Converse sneakers, I get it.

I brush my hair out of my eyes. "Well, I'm back," I say. As if he hasn't known my exact whereabouts. The man is a detective, for heaven's sake. "Been back awhile."

Bobbie has watched the exchange and apparently decided she's given Drew all the time he deserves. "And we've got work to do, so..." she says, grabbing my arm and giving Drew a little two-fingered wave goodbye.

As I back up a foot or two, the store manager sees his chance and places himself in front of Drew, trying to get his attention. Maybe what makes Drew such a good detective is his ability to focus.

Only what he's focusing on is me.

"Phone broken? Carrier pigeon died?" he asks me, taking in Fran, the manager, the meat counter and that Employees Only door, all without taking his eyes off me.

Mark tries to break the spell. "We've got work to do there, you've got work to do here, Scoones," Mark says to him, gesturing toward next door. "So it's back to the alley for us."

Drew's lip twitches. "You working the alley now?" he says.

"If you'd like to follow me," Bill-the-manager, clearly exasperated, says to Drew—who doesn't respond. It's as if waiting for my answer is all he has to do.

So, fine. "You knew I was back," I say.

The man has known my whereabouts every hour of the day for as long as I've known him. And my mother's not the only one who won't buy that he "just happened" to answer this particular call. In fact, I'm willing to bet my children's lunch money that he's taken every call within ten miles of my home since the day I got back.

And now he's gotten lucky.

"*You* could have called *me*," I say.

"You're the one who said *tomorrow* for our talk and then flew the coop, chickie," he says. "I figured the ball was in your court."

"Detective?" the uniform says. "There's something you ought to see in here."

Drew gives me a look that amounts to *in or out?*

He could be talking about the investigation, or about our relationship.

Bobbie tries to steer me away. Mark's fists are balled. Drew waits me out, knowing I won't be able to resist what might be a murder investigation.

Finally he turns and heads for the cooler.

And, like a puppy dog, I follow.

Bobbie grabs the back of my shirt and pulls me to a halt.

"I'm just going to show him something," I say, yanking away.

"Yeah," Bobbie says, pointedly looking at the buttons on my blouse. The two at breast level have popped. "That's what I'm afraid of."

HARLEQUIN®

Mediterranean NIGHTS™

*Glamour, elegance, mystery and revenge
aboard the high seas...*

Coming in August 2007...

THE TYCOON'S SON

*by
award-winning author*

Cindy Kirk

Businessman Theo Catomeris's long-estranged
father is determined to reconnect with his son, so
he hires Trish Melrose to persuade Theo to renew
his contract with Liberty Line. Sailing aboard the
luxurious *Alexandra's Dream* is a rare opportunity for
the single mom to mix business and pleasure. But
an undeniable attraction between Trish and Theo is
distracting her from the task at hand....

www.eHarlequin.com

HM38962

REQUEST YOUR FREE BOOKS!

2 FREE NOVELS PLUS 2 FREE GIFTS!

Silhouette® Romantic

SUSPENSE

Sparked by Danger, Fueled by Passion!

YES! Please send me 2 FREE Silhouette® Romantic Suspense novels and my 2 FREE gifts. After receiving them, if I don't wish to receive any more books, I can return the shipping statement marked "cancel." If I don't cancel, I will receive 4 brand-new novels every month and be billed just $4.24 per book in the U.S., or $4.99 per book in Canada, plus 25¢ shipping and handling per book plus applicable taxes, if any*. That's a savings of at least 15% off the cover price! I understand that accepting the 2 free books and gifts places me under no obligation to buy anything. I can always return a shipment and cancel at any time. Even if I never buy another book from Silhouette, the two free books and gifts are mine to keep forever.

240 SDN EEX6 340 SDN EEYJ

Name	(PLEASE PRINT)
Address	Apt. #
City	State/Prov. Zip/Postal Code

Signature (if under 18, a parent or guardian must sign)

Mail to the **Silhouette Reader Service™**:
IN U.S.A.: P.O. Box 1867, Buffalo, NY 14240-1867
IN CANADA: P.O. Box 609, Fort Erie, Ontario L2A 5X3

Not valid to current Silhouette Intimate Moments subscribers.

Want to try two free books from another line?
Call 1-800-873-8635 or visit www.morefreebooks.com.

* Terms and prices subject to change without notice. NY residents add applicable sales tax. Canadian residents will be charged applicable provincial taxes and GST. This offer is limited to one order per household. All orders subject to approval. Credit or debit balances in a customer's account(s) may be offset by any other outstanding balance owed by or to the customer. Please allow 4 to 6 weeks for delivery.

Your Privacy: Silhouette is committed to protecting your privacy. Our Privacy Policy is available online at www.eHarlequin.com or upon request from the Reader Service. From time to time we make our lists of customers available to reputable firms who may have a product or service of interest to you. If you would prefer we not share your name and address, please check here. ☐

SRS07

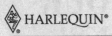

HARLEQUIN®

American ROMANCE®

TEXAS LEGACIES: *THE* CARRIGANS

Get to the Heart of a Texas Family

WITH

THE RANCHER NEXT DOOR
by
Cathy Gillen Thacker

She'll Run The Ranch—And Her Life—Her Way!

On her alpaca ranch in Texas, Rebecca encounters
constant interference from Trevor McCabe, the
bossy rancher next door. Rebecca becomes very
friendly with Vince Owen, her other neighbor and
Trevor's archrival from college. Trevor's problem
is convincing Rebecca that he is on her side, and
aware of Vince's ulterior motives. But Trevor has
fallen for her in the process....

On sale July 2007

REASONS FOR REVENGE

A brand-new provocative miniseries by *USA TODAY*
bestselling author **Maureen Child** begins with

SCORNED
BY THE BOSS

Jefferson Lyon is a man used to having his own way.
He runs his shipping empire from California, and
his admin Caitlyn Monroe runs the rest of his world.
When Caitlin decides she's had enough and needs
new scenery, Jefferson devises a plan to get her back.
Jefferson *never* loses, but little does he know that
he's in a competition....

Don't miss any of the other titles from the
REASONS FOR REVENGE trilogy by
USA TODAY bestselling author **Maureen Child.**

SCORNED BY THE BOSS #1816
Available August 2007

SEDUCED BY THE RICH MAN #1820
Available September 2007

CAPTURED BY THE BILLIONAIRE #1826
Available October 2007

Only from Silhouette Desire!

COMING NEXT MONTH

#1475 HIGH-STAKES HONEYMOON—RaeAnne Thayne
Olivia Lambert is having one hell of a honeymoon. As if being groomless
wasn't bad enough, now she's been kidnapped by a handsome stranger
claiming there's a ransom for her life! How is she supposed to trust a man
she just met, a man who has threatened her and dragged her across the
open ocean—a man who stirs a desire she never felt before?

#1476 SECRET AGENT REUNION—Caridad Piñeiro
Mission: Impassioned
A mysterious betrayal led super spy Danielle Moore to fake her own
death. Now she is ready to re-emerge and seek vengeance. But things get
complicated when she realizes a mole in her agency is still leaking vital
information—and her new partner is the ex-lover she thought dead.

#1477 THE MEDUSA AFFAIR—Cindy Dees
The Medusa Project
When Misty Cordell hears a distress call over her radio, little does she
realize a three-hour flight is about to turn into the adventure of a lifetime.
"Greg" Harkov has been leading a double life as a spy for too long and
discovers Misty could be his key out. But can he trust her with his life…
and his heart?

#1478 DANGER AT HER DOOR—Beth Cornelison
A journalist hungry for his big break gets the story of a lifetime when a
once-closed rape case resurfaces…and the victim is none other than his
reclusive neighbor. But Jack Calhoun wasn't expecting the onslaught of
attraction for Megan, or the urge to protect her.